THE
SUMMIT

THE
SUMMIT

JOURNEY TO
HERO MOUNTAIN

AN ALLEGORY

DEBORAH JOHNSON

To my sons and their families who are climbing their own summits. It is a joy for me to watch them on their journeys.

Acknowledgements

I have not climbed my Summit alone, so I appreciate those who have been with me on my journey of writing, crafting, and creating this book. Jen Singer, thank you for your abilities as a developmental editor. You chopped, refined, and pushed me to *show, not tell.* I am grateful for the readers who gave me the gift of their time and voices to help me cut, hone, and expand the manuscript: Cathy, Janet, Doug, Sandra, Caryn, Paula, and Greg.

My thanks also go to those who have been with me on my life's journey, my lifetime group: Marcia, Peggy, and JoAnne, I love and appreciate them so much. We have been together for many years and continue to laugh, cry, and pray for each other. Paula Miller, thank you for stepping in to add your additional editing touches to further enhance and format this manuscript and for all your input on many of my previous projects.

In loving memory of my parents, I miss you every day, Mom and Dad. You have now reached your heavenly Summit, and the longer I am on my life's journey, I find more ways that you have paved the way for me. I am so grateful, especially for the faith you instilled in me that has made such a difference in my life. For my family, including our sons, spouses, and grandkids, I find such joy in praying for you. I follow your journeys and nod my head silently when I need to keep my mouth shut, just as my daddy did.

Finally, my thanks go to my husband Greg, my lifetime companion and love. As we journey together through our second half, my love for you grows stronger and deeper. Your encouragement and love for me are worth more than all the jewels I could ever find. You are a gift in my life.

Contents

The Summit is the story of Mallery, a young woman who hides her ideas in a book beneath her pillow.

She decides to escape the constraints of the land of Baybel to pursue her Summit, which holds the promise of a bigger and better future. She crosses multiple terrains, mountainous caverns, and rocky hills. Along the way, she discovers her keys of courage and gems of opportunity, learning that she has everything within her to press on to reach the very top.

Mallery, which means "the unfortunate and insignificant one," uses her Band of Hope to affirm her ideas, strengths, and uniqueness to set her apart from the ordinary. She emerges from the tangled forest, cave of discovery, and bridge of possibility strong and fearless, ready to meet her future.

The Summit is an entertaining allegory that inspires us to reach the Summit of our own Hero Mountain, never losing hope in "The Hero Inside" all of us.

CHAPTER ONE

The Timely Offer

In the family cottage at the foot of rolling green hills, Mallery hid her ideas in a book she kept in a satchel beneath her pillow. This book held the dreams she had stopped sharing after her mother told her, "Get your head out of the clouds and get to your chores like everyone else in Baybel!" Their simple home looked like many other cottages in their little village, with enough space for herself, her sister Cagney and brother Treston. Her room, though, was a converted closet, so small that her bed was built into a wall. In fact, everything about her life seemed small.

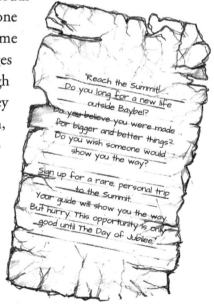

"Reach the Summit!
Do you long for a new life outside Baybel?
Do you believe you were made for bigger and better things?
Do you wish someone would show you the way?

Sign up for a rare, personal trip to the Summit.
Your guide will show you the way.
But hurry. This opportunity is only good until The Day of Jubilee."

Mallery daydreamed about what would happen if she followed her dreams. Then people would look up to her, admiring

1

her accomplishments. But whenever her ideas were met with a furrowed brow or a tsk-tsk, she retreated further into herself until soon, she, too, grew critical of her own ideas. She'd learned the hard way what happened when she shared her ideas with others.

"You and your crazy dreams," her father often chastised her.

"That's not how the world works, Mallery," her teacher told her. "Better to stick to safe plans that have worked for other people."

"Did you really think that was a good idea? Ha!" Her brother Treston laughed at her.

After achieving several certificates, Mallery took a job as an accountant, a "safe" position by Baybel standards, leaving her closet bedroom and family cottage behind. Once in her own small apartment, she could see the possibilities clearly like sunshine through glass. So she kept writing her dreams, her pen scrawling the words, *I just know some of my dreams have potential!* She pictured herself standing at a podium before hundreds of people – her people – leading and motivating them to work on her ideas and creations.

"Today is the day we've all been waiting for," she would announce, "breaking ground on our newly designed community center!" The thunderous applause in her imagination was cut short when her faithful companion Crockett barked for attention.

A clear vision required an action plan. Badly wanting success, she turned to others for opinions and feedback. Surely coworkers and friends would know better than she did how to begin. She took advice and tried emulating those she admired, but copying others only brought discouragement. For example, her friend Tamma, whose name means "perfect one," always looked put-together – polished makeup, lovely long hair, glowing personality. Even her social media posts, issued multiple times a day, appeared astute. Tamma had this annoying knack of turning every picture into a flawless image with an endearing meme.

Mallery, meanwhile, struggled with a few extra pounds that, technically, didn't make her overweight, but made her curvy in all the wrong places. She thought, *Maybe if I was a little thinner or had the*

right clothes. Yes, that's it. I've always heard you should dress for success.
Consequently, Mallery created some self-portraits to announce herself
to the world. She found, on sale, the kind of outfit Tamma might
wear, then had her hair and makeup done professionally. Yet when
the finished photos arrived, she felt devastated.

"I look dumpy," she told Crockett. "I'll never be one of the beautiful people, and only they rule the world."

A short time later, Mallery found a flyer tacked to the announcement board in town:

Reach the Summit!

Do you long for a new life outside Baybel?
Do you believe you were made for bigger and better things?
Do you wish someone would show you the way?

Sign up for a rare, personal trip to the Summit.
Your guide will show you the way.
But hurry. This opportunity is only good until The Day of Jubilee.

She had seen many glossy ads and eye-catching photos touting tours
that could take individuals to the Summit. However, this one sounded
different, with a personal guide and a deadline just days away.

Other villagers she knew seemed to take the same route, and as a
result, the people appeared unchanged by their journeys upon returning. Plus, she never knew if they actually got to the Summit, as their
excursions seemed to be quite short. She just took it for granted when
they spoke about it, each trying to outdo the other's story. But she
thought it should be a longer journey, one that included places and
events that would bring about a bigger and better future. Maybe they
took shortcuts?

Her days and nights became filled with thoughts about the guided
journey, and she mentioned it to Crockett, her faithful "explorer" dog,

who opened an eye, then went back to his slumbering bliss. She rolled over and pulled out her book of ideas. Every single project had flopped or remained untried because she'd listened to the feedback from people who'd never had an original idea or even thought about taking a journey to the Summit. She pulled out her book: *I'd love to go to the Summit to find out who I could really become.*

She took out her savings, a bag of coins and bills. Would it be enough to pay the guide? Her mother would view it as Mallery wasting her money on foolishness, but something about the flyer and the guided journey spoke to her. The deadline, The Day of Jubilee, gave her an excuse to miss the event. Last year's Jubilee had featured a talent competition that had been the most embarrassing episode of her life. She never wanted to go again. The Summit was her opportunity to escape. That thought helped her sleep. Hours later, she woke up with questions.

"Do I have what it takes to reach the Summit? What if I stumble? What if I fail? Will this guide help me?" Crockett didn't stir. "Oh Crockett, I've got to stop fretting." Mallery's fear of not measuring up started as far back as grade school when her mother discouraged a friendship with a smart classmate who lived across town.

"You're not in her league," her mother told her. "People like us can't just push our way into their world, can we? You will never measure up to your friend, anyway. So stop trying."

As Crockett lifted his head, Mallery made a decision. "I need to talk to the guide. If I don't, I may never have this opportunity again."

She was sure many had seen the invitation. So how would that guide have the time to take her call? Still, she summoned up the courage to dial the number. To her surprise, someone answered, "Hello."

"This is Mallery. I'm calling about the Summit trip. I ... I've had friends do Summit trips, but nothing really changed for them. Is this one different?"

She felt a little strange asking the big question right off and spoke more quickly than usual, but the guide didn't seem to mind.

"This trip is unlike the others," he explained. "It won't be easy. But, despite some steep mountains, slippery slopes, and dangerous rocks, you will have everything you need to be successful."

"I'm not strong or athletic and definitely not a climber. What if I fall? How will this trip help me get where I want to go?"

"This trip will only help if you decide to go. I can only assist if you are committed. I will be walking with you some of the way, but for the most part, you will make the journey on your own."

"Wait a minute. You're not going to be with me the whole way?" When her friends talked about their summits, they made it all look easy, but this sounded hard. If she failed, the whole town would know.

He replied, "You will get tools for each part of your climb."

"Do you mean walking sticks and stuff like that?"

"You'll have guidance for your decisions as well as tools." He added, "One more thing: when you reach the Summit, your name will change."

She remembered how her friends would tease about her name, chanting, "Mallery, Mallery, you're ill-fated! Even your name is under-stated." Her mother thought it was a pretty name even though it meant "unfortunate." Still, Mallery worried about what everyone would think, most of all her mother, if she changed her name. As if reading her thoughts, the guide added, "It's a condition of the climb. You can't return from the Summit without changing your name."

"But all my friends came back with the same names."

"Not everybody has what it takes to complete *this* climb. Give me your decision by midnight."

As the call ended, Mallery turned to her dog. "Midnight? What should I do, Crockett?" Just saying the words comforted her, though she did wish her dog could, in some way, answer. Her phone beeped with the name "Craven" on the screen. She knew her cousin could not aid her in her decision making, though they had done a lot together through the years. They had developed a bond, both being afraid of anything that sniffed of danger, like diving off a rock into a pond during a family reunion. Though the pond was plenty deep, and the rock was merely a few feet off the ground, they chose not to jump.

Ignoring his call, she sat down by Crockett. "I want to say 'yes,' but I'm afraid. I rescued you, Crockett. Maybe you can rescue me." With this, the dog laid his head in her lap. "I will go, but only if you're my companion." As she petted his head, he whimpered, which she took as a "Yes." Summoning her courage, she contacted the guide.

"I will ... I mean, I've decided to go."

"I'm happy for you, Mallery. I will send a list of items to bring and the location for departure. See you first thing tomorrow. Also, do not tell anyone else of your journey, at least not yet. They may try to dissuade you."

When she hung up, Craven's name appeared again on her phone. She imagined him sitting in his room, alone among friends. At least he called them "friends," the ones who played the same online games, all safely cocooned behind their computer screens. She answered, knowing he'd worry if she didn't.

"Mallery! I've been calling you all day."

"I've been busy!"

"Too busy to take my call? That's not like you! Do you want to come with me tonight?"

"Where?" she laughed.

"The festival talent competition! You were a huge hit last year!" Craven rarely went out these days, so she was surprised he was even going.

"Are you kidding?"

"No! It was the funniest act in the whole program! Remember the applause?"

Mallery remembered the laughter and jeers as she tripped off the stage. She had been talked into singing her parody of a popular disco song, "I Have Arrived." Forgetting half the lyrics, she left the platform, humiliated. "No way will I ever do that again."

Don't be so hard on yourself! The competition is the main event at The Jubilee, besides all the good food and free stuff, that is. C'mon, join me!"

"I can't. I'm getting ready for a trip."

"Where?"

"To the Summit. Leaving tomorrow."

"You? Trying to climb the Summit? Ha! What about the danger? I'd never do it. I'm surprised you'd even think about it!"

"I hear it's not easy, but I've decided."

"Not easy? That's an understatement. Mallery, we've talked about risks before. You and I, we aren't in the same league as those who climb the mountain peaks. We like safe valleys."

"Craven, you sound like my mom!"

"You're not strong enough! Who's going to help you?"

"I've hired a guide. I'm going now. Goodbye, Craven." Self-doubt flooded her mind. Worse yet she'd told a family member about her plan. Soon, they'd all know. "What was I thinking? Maybe Craven is right?" Crockett raised an eyebrow. She snuggled in the corner with him, his steady breathing calming her and bringing her sleep.

CHAPTER TWO

The Arrangement

Mallery woke up feeling anxious, but the sun boosted her spirits as it boldly made its multi-hued appearance with vibrant shades of orange, pink, and yellow. She got up, turned off her phone, and finished packing. "Now, what will you need, Crockett? I'll take plenty of doggie bones!" As she put dog treats in her suitcase, she cleared her mind of any recollection of last year's Jubilee performance. She left her house quietly to avoid attracting unnecessary attention and to escape her cousin Shamere, who was expected to visit.

"I think you're more excited about this trip than I am!" She responded to Crockett's prancing. "But I   definitely don't want to see Shamere this morning, especially after talking with Craven. I won't endure another round of her criticism and shaming. I don't want anything to hold me back."

She liked the cheeriness in her voice. In her quest to be more than Mallery, the ill-omened, she had often felt alone. Now with a guide to help her, a tint of optimism was coming through. As she approached the corner shop, their meeting place, she inhaled the sweet aroma of fresh coffee beans, but resisted their temptation. She couldn't carry anything extra. The snacks, water, and travel essentials in her backpack would be enough for her first day. She spotted the guide through the window. He gazed directly at Crockett. If he wouldn't let dogs go, Crockett would be her way out.

"Mallery, why did you bring your dog?"

"I want him by my side. He's a good walker, and I have everything he'll need."

"That was not our arrangement."

"I know we didn't talk about it, but I have nowhere to leave Crockett. He can't stay in my apartment by himself."

It was a long while before the guide answered. "Okay, bring Crockett, but you don't need him for the trip. You're fine by yourself." Mallery stayed silent. As if on cue, Crockett looked pleadingly at the Guide with his big brown eyes. Sighing, the guide took out a small yellow band.

"Wear this throughout your journey." He placed it on her right wrist, a perfect fit. "This is the Band of Hope. Never take it off."

"Hope?" That was just a promotional term used for face creams and new product promises. The word's meaning had faded. Was it hope that lead to Nirvana or Heaven?

"How can a simple band give me hope? It's not possible." The band slightly loosened around her wrist.

"You can't succeed without hope on your journey. Remember what you wrote about scaling your Summit?" She wondered how he knew about her journal.

"I want to find out who I can become." The Band of Hope tightened around her wrist.

"Hope will get you there." With that, the guide led the way down a road by the shop.

"This route is beautiful." The way was lined with colorful peonies, daisies, and wildflowers. She couldn't see past the hill and thick grove of trees beyond the first sharp curve, though she had heard there was a forest nearby. Now, matching her pace with the guide's, she continued, "I've never been on this road as long as I've lived here."

"You aren't the only one."

"I've heard some bad things happened in this forest, people getting lost or hurt."

"Oh, you will be perfectly safe. Just follow the path."

Now, with an optimism and assurance she had not felt in a long while, she almost leaped for joy. If this was her journey, she knew it would be successful, particularly with a competent guide. Adventure was invigorating, especially when surrounded by such beauty.

Back home, it didn't take long for the news to spill out all over town about her trip. Craven made sure of that. Her phone pinged several times with social media messages, announcing her journey.

"Who did you tell about your trip, Mallery?"

How to answer the guide? Mallery knew she needed to be truthful. "Craven called me, and I didn't want to accompany him to the Festival talent competition."

"So you told him you were going to the Summit?"

"I didn't think it mattered. Craven is fearful like me. I mean, he won't do anything but talk."

"By sharing your plans, you have given power to those who don't want you to make your Summit. I warned you not to talk, at least not yet."

"I did stand up to him," she replied. "I dismissed his comments." She felt her elation for the journey slipping.

As they entered the first grove of trees, the guide said, "I will be leaving you for a time."

"Already? We just started! Who will I lean on if I get lost or encounter danger?" Directions were not easy for her. Was Craven right? Maybe she couldn't make this trip. What was she thinking? She stopped in her tracks, frozen by her thoughts.

"Just stay on the path. Don't fear. I won't be far away if you need help. Use your phone for emergencies, but don't answer any calls from home. Like Craven's call, they will only distract, dissuade, and discourage you."

"But what if my friends get worried about me?"

"Since when have they *really* been worried about you? How long has it been since anyone asked you about your ideas, plans, or dreams?"

"I can't remember."

"You will be fine without answering distracting calls."

With slow breaths, she started moving, and Crockett rose to follow.

The guide continued, "Once you let in a seed of doubt, it will continue growing unless you keep going toward your goal."

Mallery knew he was right. Even though she wondered if Craven would be hiding beyond the first bend, coming out from his online adventures to scare her, she didn't want her suspicions to keep her from reaching her goal.

"I thought you'd be with me longer, at least at first."

"You'll be fine. Just stay on the path." With that, the Guide stooped to gently rub Crockett's head and said goodbye.

Mallery stepped into the large grove of trees, which suddenly looked like a dense, fully-grown forest. With the ground firm and the trail clear, she was happy to see that it was easy to follow the path.

"Crockett, look how beautiful the forest is!" Indifferent, Crockett lunged at a rabbit that crossed his path. Mallery pulled back on the leash. "How could a place this lovely be dangerous?"

A choir of birds sang overhead, all in different keys, volume, and timbre. It reminded her of the classical recordings her mother had played while she was growing up. The music of Puccini, Debussy, Schubert, and others were beautiful to her ears. Her heart sang along; she felt like skipping as she inhaled the scent of damp moss and pine trees. Her journey was starting better than she could have imagined, as she didn't even feel alone. Yet as she looked ahead, the pathway suddenly ended with nothing in view beyond the next curve.

CHAPTER THREE

The Tangled Forest

"He said we'd be safe," Mallery reminded herself as she neared the path's dead end. Suddenly, she jumped. A snake, wound tightly on a rock, inched forward. Carefully guiding Crockett away, she avoided the reptile. Then her phone vibrated in her pocket with Cagney's name flashing on the screen. Mallery considered, should she answer? Her sister Cagney could be encouraging in the most discouraging way, like the times the girls played tennis together. She'd tell Mallery "good shot," but then add, "Do you want feedback?" Cagney was no better at tennis than Mallery. She just *thought* she was better. Her forte was giving Mallery unwarranted and, at times, misguided instructions on any subject.

Mallery let the call go to voicemail. At the end of the path, a narrow dirt track veered left. A cheerful harmonic chorus of the birds surrounded them. As Mallery advanced, the dense growth shaded the sunlight, darkening the path yard by yard. She felt thankful for the flashlight in her pack as the way became difficult to maneuver; though surprisingly, Crockett enjoyed the challenge. When tree roots and vines jumped into the path from nowhere as if to trip or grab her, she walked even more cautiously. The last thing she needed was a twisted ankle. Farther on, she climbed atop a large rock and pulled out her snack bag. While Crockett munched a dog treat, she saw the chocolate chip crunch crescent cookies she had impulsively packed. Digging further, she decided on a healthier choice of a trail mix. "I hope these last longer than an afternoon, Crockett!"

Meanwhile, back in Baybel, Cagney grew concerned when her calls to Mallery went unanswered. Wasn't Mallery always available for a chat? In desperation, Cagney dialed Craven.

"She's heading to the Summit," Craven announced, as he dropped his phone and fumbled to pick it up.

"Why? She's not the type to complete anything, let alone a long journey. She could get hurt up there! I'm calling Treston." Once Treston picked up, Cagney gave him the news.

"I've been in that forest," Treston said. "It's no place for Mallery." Cagney wondered what help Treston would be though. He'd once led his entire cross country team down the wrong trail in a major race, disqualifying them all. He wasn't exactly a good leader. Still, he held a high opinion of himself, even greater than Cagney's ego.

"You've gone to the forest?"

"Many times!" he exaggerated. "I went in just to show my fraidy-cat pals it could be done." He laughed, "They're still too chicken to try!"

"In that case, you'd better hurry! She may be in trouble!"

Treston, immediately regretting his decision, reasoned that Mallery would not be that far on her journey. He imagined her perched on a rock, eating all her food in one sitting. After all, she always stood first in the food line at their family picnics.

"She's probably on her way back already. But I 'll check. Treston to the rescue!" With his custom running shoes, he could easily outpace Mallery, the stubborn girl who didn't even own sneakers. At one time, she had helped him promote all his race wins, but she stopped suddenly once she started writing her own articles. Treston quickly rounded the first bend on the forest trail, then slowed, frustrated by the tangled vines and roots in his path. Before long, he yelled, "Mallery! Mallery! Eating already?"

"Treston, what are you doing here?" Mallery looked up in disbelief.

"Cagney and I got worried about you! You're crazy to hike out here." At that, Crockett barked and nipped at Treston's feet. Jumping aside, he almost kicked the dog. The birds squawked angrily, swooping at his head.

"You think that dog will protect you? Or these obnoxious birds?" He took her hands in his. "I'll take you back to town and help you over these troublesome roots. It will only get harder if you keep going!"

Mallery had never seen her brother show such concern before. As she stared at his angular face, his left cheek twitched slightly. She could see that the forward track did look more difficult as the knotted vines grew denser and the way narrowed further.

"I know it's hard," she protested.

"Ha! Hard?" His toothy smile reminded her of a neighbor's Shetland Pony, and his twitch became more apparent. "I know you, Mallery. You care about our family. Think of our mother. She'll be worried sick!"

"Mom knows?"

"Probably!"

Now, Mallery knew she'd never live it down if she didn't make the Summit. Bad news would travel fast, making her feel even more like a loser. Treston, letting go of her hands, paced in a circle. It reminded her of the time he mocked her, reading aloud a rejection letter she'd once gotten from a publisher.

"Remember how you ridiculed me when the publisher rejected my article?"

"Someone had to tell you to quit writing those articles. It was just tough love."

"It hurt, and you were wrong."

She had felt elated coming into the forest, but now her confidence struggle resurfaced. The deep seed of hurt he had caused had only grown, festering into an annoying boil. No wonder the guide told her not to talk to anyone from home.

"I need to talk to my guide before doing anything else. He will know what to do!" Crockett barked in affirmation. Treston drew his face close enough for her to smell his garlic breath. He had probably eaten a large lunch, so her stomach growled in response.

"Ha! Your guide? Same old Mallery still can't decide for herself!"

Suddenly, she heard a rustle in the leaves, and her guide stood before her. Treston jumped back with eyes widening and gasping like a hot balloon releasing its air.

"Mallery, I'll see you at home." Then, to the guide, he said, "Stop brainwashing my sister!"

The next moment, he abruptly turned, heading toward home. He picked up speed and stumbled over the vines, as if running away. The guide gave a treat to Crockett.

"Did you tell Treston you were on a climb to your Summit?"

"No, but maybe my cousin did."

"Such interference will make the journey more difficult, but you will become stronger as you overcome each obstacle. Or have you changed your mind?"

"Oh no. I just didn't realize what was involved."

"No one does who *truly* makes it to the Summit, but you will succeed. Some people claim they care about you, even family members. Unfortunately, though, they're led by self-interest. Treston doesn't want to be embarrassed by the possibility of your failure. He wants to be the family rescuer."

"Yes, he always tries to save the day!"

"Questioning your brother's criticism was a step in the right direction. By doing so, you affirmed your abilities. That will lead to your growth."

"By just bringing it up?"

"Yes, you affirmed how his comments discouraged you from writing. Your healthy self-talk and language are tools you will need. Now you can pick up your pen again."

The guide was right. She had nothing to prove to Treston or anyone else.

"You will be tested, but you can get to the Summit."

"Is that why the Band of Hope feels warm on my wrist?"

"It will remind you of your purpose throughout your journey. Never take it off."

"What if I lose it?"

But the guide had already left. She wondered what enchanted power lived in the simple band.

"Let's go, Crockett!" He took his place in front of her, leading through twist and turns of the trail as vines and roots grew thicker and difficult to avoid. She stumbled a few times, remembering how she had twisted her ankle on the tennis court. Recovery time could impede her progress, so she could not risk an injury.

Rounding a large bend, she stopped in her tracks. Ahead, the road divided. "We have a choice to make all ready? I thought the path would be clear." Even in their small town, she had taken wrong turns, feeling lost. It was especially frightening at night in areas with few lights and fewer signs. Now, with the impending darkness, she stepped slowly toward one of the trails. Suddenly, Crockett barked.

"What do you see, Boy?" Focusing her eyes beyond the tangled branches, a thin line of smoke rose above the trees to her right. She smelled wood burning. "Who would live out here?" Trusting the guide's words that she'd be safe, she moved to check out a log cabin in the distance, unsure what she would encounter. Still, her hunger drove her forward, and sleeping in the wild in the small tent held no appeal. Crockett led her to the front door. She knocked, but there was no answer. When she tried the handle, the door creaked open.

"Ah!" Just the sight of a blazing fireplace made her feel comfortable and secure. Crockett, spotting a dog bed, curled up to claim his territory. "Wait, Crockett! We need to find out who lives here." A place setting for one lay on the table with food already prepared. "The inhabitant might be back any minute." Crockett didn't move. A cot with a down comforter sat in the corner.

"This must be a secret hideaway. Why would someone leave a hot meal here if he wasn't coming right back?" She inhaled the food's delicious aroma as steam rose from the plate. A note on the edge of the table caught her eye: "For MAL."

> Welcome, Mallery! I'm so glad you are my guest tonight. Your guide told me you were coming. Please enjoy your dinner and sleep well. Also, you'll find extra food and water for Crockett by the front door.

As if on cue, Crockett rose and started eating.

"If you're going to eat, so am I." This situation seemed too good to be true. After a few delicious bites, she noticed a small notebook on the table. It was cloth covered with designs of leaves and foliage. The green reminded her of the forest right outside the door. She read the inscription:

> This is the journal you will write in every day. Maybe just two lines, or a couple of pages. Your writing will help you sort out your thoughts, strategies, and actions. The words you record will keep you focused and will document your trip so you will never forget the lessons you have learned along the way. Thoughts become clearer as you state and then communicate them.

She ate a few more bites. Crockett, already finished, curled up in his bed. Then she picked up the pen and wrote her first entry:

Stepping around a snake today in the forest felt challenging enough, but the hardest part of my trip so far has been facing my feelings of inadequacy. The guide was there for me when I needed him, but I didn't realize what would be involved in this journey. Seeing my brother reminded me how easily I gave up on writing. He has power to discourage me when I least expect it. I don't want to give up on the things I love. I want to grow stronger.

She closed the journal, finished dinner, and cleaned the plates. In front of the fire, the surging flames lulled her into a hypnotic state as the blaze slowly died. Choosing the next path could wait until morning. As soon as she lay on the cot, she fell fast asleep.

The next morning, she found yogurt, berries, granola, juice, and a roll waiting for her in the small refrigerator, along with food for Crockett, which he gulped down. There was also a small bag with snacks for the day. She ate heartily, then put her newly acquired journal in her backpack, and left the cottage that had been so welcoming on her first night. On the trail, two divergent paths lay before her, but the morning light revealed more detail. Squinting, she made out a sign at the crest of the first turn on the wider path. "Crockett, is that a Dead-End sign?" In response, the dog pulled her toward the opposite path, which was narrower and overgrown with dense snarling masses of roots and vines.

"What are you doing? Where's your sense of direction? This is obviously the harder route. Did you see something?" He jumped over some jagged rocks, pulling her along. "Well, I guess I have no choice. At least there's no Dead-End sign ahead." Stumbling forward, she called, "Slow down. I'm not a wagon train. What are you so excited about?" She held the leash taut. The chorus of bird songs grew louder and more intense, as if they were singing just to her.

"To think, Treston called these noisy birds! I love them." Crockett tried catching one, jumping up when one flew low. The Band of Hope felt firm on her wrist, assuring her that she was on the right path, even though the darkness created by the thick mass of trees made it difficult to tell how much time passed. By noon, she saw a clearing ahead. A beam of light through the trees broke through the density, which was a welcome sight.

Crockett wanted to run, but she held him back, taking deliberate steps. The snake they had seen the previous day reminded her how important it was to stay alert. It would be easy to let her guard down, but after the surprise visit from her brother, she had the feeling she'd need to be extra alert for the unexpected.

"We are on our way to the Summit, Crockett!" Just hearing herself say those words gave her an unexpected burst of hope. "Actually, we're on our way to *my* Summit." That personalization sounded even better to her, though she knew her traveling companion was just along for the adventure and maybe a few extra treats. The path brought her toward the expanding light, but she still wasn't out of the forest. The edge of the tree line lay ahead. Where was her Summit? Was it a mountain or just a figurative peak? Soon she would know.

CHAPTER FOUR

The Keys of Courage

The valley ahead was a welcome sight. Mallery stretched her arms to the sky as if to release her thoughts from the dark, dense jungle overgrowth. Emerging from shadows into the sunshine reminded her of rainy days when she was young and how nice it was to finally play outside. It didn't matter how cold or warm the temperature. She had always loved watching the roly-polies and earthworms emerge, slithering through the dirt, doing their mundane, but important jobs. She remembered the uninhibited freedom of running and jumping, getting away from the confines of her classroom desk. As an adult, she felt the same way when she got away from her cubicle at work. She tried to sneak out for short walks often. Now, Crockett ran through some

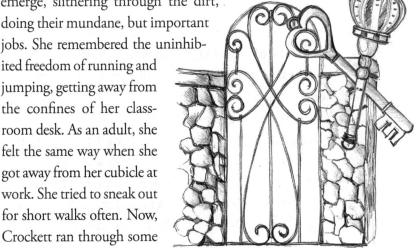

23

tall grass, momentarily free from his leash as he stirred up butterflies and a loud squawking bird that teased him along.

Taking some spins herself, the bright sun warmed her back. She looked ahead at the outlines of what seemed like large anthills. As she came closer, the hills in the horizon appeared uniform, the size of small bunkers in half-domed shapes, formed too perfectly to be a part of the natural landscape. Crockett continued running circles around her, but she got his attention by bribing him with a bone. Then, she took out the small pita bread sandwich, also included that morning in her provisions. Amazingly, it contained some of her favorite extras like sprouts and cheeses. She had not shared any diet preferences with her guide, so how did he know what foods she liked?

She wanted a map, as she felt more secure knowing where she was going. As Mallery and Crockett advanced along the route, the hills grew larger and some contained cave-like entryways that looked ample enough to crawl through. She stopped to try one of the doors, but it did not budge. She remembered, at the local animal shelter, how the animals practically jumped out of their cages toward her as she passed by. Was something dangerous locked behind these mysterious doors? She pulled Crockett along on his leash, hastening her pace. The bunkers, increasing in size, stood high enough for a person to enter. But was it safe? If she got trapped in one, no one would find her – ever. Then, Treston's prediction would come true. A key was attached to a lock on the door handle of a bunker just ahead. "Could this be a test, Crockett?" If what was inside was truly dreadful, what would she do?

"Oh, why did I listen to Craven or Treston?" Just the thought of them brought up their warnings about terrible misfortunes that could happen to her. As a result, she remained hypervigilant of potential danger. She recalled her recent journal entry: *I don't want to give up on this trip. I want to be stronger than that.* Mallery summoned her inner resolve, boosted by her curiosity, and put her hand on the key. She felt the Band of Hope warm on her wrist. She inched closer to read the etched inscription that read: "I Can."

That phrase "I can" was not spoken often in Baybel, at least not among her friends and family. She couldn't remember ever saying those words to herself and meaning them. Her mantra had often been, "I can't." She declined creative activities that could garner criticism, especially her brother's. Yet her guide had mentioned that healthy self-talk and language are the tools she would need. Anything could be behind a door with an "I Can" key attached to it. If it held some secret significance, she had to find out.

"Sit, Crockett." She grabbed the lock and tried the key saying, "I can." With a single turn, the door swung wide with a pop. Crockett barked as she jumped back. When nothing moved, she peered inside. A note hung from a silver pouch:

Along your journey, hold this pouch. Then use all the keys you find to unlock the potential of your mind.

"Potential of my mind?" This note had to be for someone else. "Potential" was another word she only heard once or twice, once from a teacher long ago. Mallery had won a week's worth of popcorn when her model of a Peruvian village won first prize in a seventh-grade geography contest. Yet her mother had not been happy because Mallery had used all the flour and salt for the homemade dough so that her mother didn't have enough ingredients to make cookies for her social event that night.

Mallery took the bag, placing the "I Can" key inside. Holding on to a key seemed like a strange request, but if this was truly for her, there must be a reason. The next bunker key also had an inscription: "I Will." Those words were more familiar to her. She said them to herself and to her guide when starting this venture. She even remembered saying the words to Craven when he called. She felt empowered in a small way as she placed this key in her silver bag.

She found a third key with the inscription "Courage." It made her step back momentarily. She knew that a person must face her fears to have courage, but she feared rejection, and that had kept her from taking risks. Would taking this key help her venture into areas where she was uncomfortable? With all the put-downs she had experienced through the years for everything from creative financing to a community project, this key seemed to carry peril. It was easier to stay safely out of criticism's way. However, she re-read the note included with the pouch:

> Use all the keys you find to unlock the potential
> of your mind.

"All" didn't mean "some," so its message urged her conscience to dutifully put the key in her silver pouch.

The next key said, "Confidence." She let out a deep, exasperating breath, another tough one. She failed miserably in trying to live up to Tamma's "perfect" image. Comparison had become her evil companion as she measured her life with the imaginary success of others. Even her well-meaning family, who said they cared for her, rarely asked about her plans. When meeting someone new, she easily sank into invisibility, as others talked endlessly about their own goals and achievements. Who had told her that if she faced obstacles with courage, her confidence would grow? Despite misgivings, she wondered if she could find courage. The key went in her bag.

The last key, "Joy," made her wonder if she could escape her lonely dilemma and the semi-depression and gloomy outlook that she had endured for so long. However, just seeing the word "Joy" proved comforting. Cagney, Mallery's sister, served as a cautionary example, for her own dreary life had crippled her so that she hardly ventured from home. She lived a bleak, trapped existence, the essence of her name. Consequently, Cagney wanted to transfer that identity to Mallery. Resisting that snare had motivated Mallery to take this trip. With all five keys secured inside the pouch, she wondered what secrets they would unlock. The keys held unique designs, good to keep as mementos of her adventure. Clutching the bag gave her a warm feeling as she stroked the Band of Hope that had grown tighter on her wrist. Was hope's message starting to rub off on her?

Crockett's bark brought her back to reality. As they rounded the next curve, she saw her guide! Overjoyed, she almost dropped the leash. Her words poured out in a jumble, "What are these keys for? Why do I need them? Are they really for me? Can I keep them? Is there a gate somewhere?"

Laughing, he gave Crockett a treat, which the dog gobbled down. "I'm glad you're so excited, especially about the keys. You will use them all."

"All?" Mallery felt slightly disappointed. She had already imagined how nice they would look hanging on her wall at home.

"They will unlock the gates before you."

"Is there a map? Will I start climbing soon?"

"You will be climbing soon enough, but some areas you need to pass through first to prepare."

"To be honest, I feel a bit lost."

"Trust that you will have everything you need to proceed."

"I've had some not-so-good experiences with trust."

"That's because you're not trusting what is trustworthy. Some people, even your friends who said they'd be there for you, will let you down."

"Yes, and that hurts." She paused, feeling safe enough to share. "I stood up for one of my colleagues at work on a submitted financial document, but he totally changed his tune, making me look naive and untrustworthy."

"Trouble happens, but this journey will grow your trust. Don't be afraid. You found everything you needed last night, didn't you?"

"It was wonderful! Thank you."

"A gate in front of Cyber Hill is just ahead. One of your keys will fit. Other gates will follow, so use all the keys to gain access."

"Why so many gates? My apartment complex only has one gate and that seems sufficient."

"There are those who try to gain access unfairly. You do remember the recent fake message you responded to about your credit account?"

"Oh yes, a huge hassle, having to change all my passwords and file multiple fraud reports."

"So part of your journey requires having multiple keys of protection. They will reinforce the language you need to ward off what is fake. Some critics will try to keep you from reaching your potential."

Mallery felt like she had come far enough so that no one from home would bother her though she still wasn't exactly sure where she was. "I never want to be hacked again, but I don't know what anyone could do to hack me out here." She almost missed his last comment as he left.

"Just be careful of whom and to what you give access."

The "I Can" key fit perfectly in the large gate before her, which closed suddenly and locked firmly behind her with a bang that made her jump and Crockett yelp. She had to trust herself. Seeing her guide intensified her resolve. She repeated, "I can, I can" to calm her nerves and strengthen her determination. The smaller gate ahead led to a garden with trees throughout. A branch containing tangelos hung over the gate close enough for her to pick one. "Yum." She ate the sweet fruit. Produce straight from the garden made her happy. Wiping her sticky fingers, she tried some keys in her pouch. The "I Will" key fit perfectly.

The words, "I won't" had been her mantra after hearing comments about her ideas. "I told you they'd never go for it," her accounting partner chided after the rejection of her new software that she knew could save the company time and money. After she had spent two years developing it, the rejection didn't just come once, but multiple times from others. Soon, she didn't even submit her ideas anymore. Saying "I will" felt like she was finally proving her detractors wrong. "I will. I will."

She wanted to spend the rest of the afternoon right there, inspecting every plant and inhaling the earthy fragrance of the citrus grove.

However, the mystery of where she would stay the night took over her thoughts. She'd need to move forward, as darkness would soon be upon her. In the large garden, she ate ripe strawberries, so when she came upon the next gate, she gasped. A thorny thistle patch had weeds almost as tall as she was. Instead of a tangelo tree, brush full of stickers had grown through the entrance. The keyhole was not visible, so she brushed the vegetation aside, but sharp thorns pricked her skin. She tried the "Confidence" key, but it did not fit. "Maybe we should just stay in the garden, Crockett. We could always pitch our tent."

But when she tried the "Courage" key, it opened the gate. It would take courage and resolve to enter this mess of ragweed and thistles. "I'm sorry Crockett. I know you're going to get thorns and thistles in your paws." As the gate swung wide, she held it as long as she could, moving ahead on the path, still clearly marked at the entrance. The gate nearly smacked them as it closed. It sounded more final than the others. Her arms itched just seeing the weeds and the thorny bushes that moved in the light breeze, aware they could jump out and scratch her at any time. As she stepped forward, the path all but disappeared. Her brother's words rang in her ears, "This is a huge mistake!" Why couldn't she put that message out of her mind? But Mallery wondered if in this situation, he was right. She was now far away from her family, friends, and even her town. After thirty minutes with no clear path, the thorns and briars had become even thicker, increasing her sense of isolation. Her guide did say to be careful of whom and to what she gave access. Was he even the right person to trust?

Stopping to pull out a sticker from Crockett's paw, she noticed her arms were covered with scratches. A particularly tall weed had jumped out and made a puncture deep enough to draw blood. Itching and shivering, she knew that if she turned back, she could at least return to the garden. That is, if she could get back through the gate. Just then, she remembered the last key, "Courage." All she had learned about courage was how easy it was to get beat up. It was less risky to let herself be bullied and beat up even by her friends and family than to answer back and face more criticism. She would cower at their comments and say nothing, seething inside, but mostly quitting. People thought she was quiet. She knew endurance and stamina were elements of being courageous. Was this the lesson she needed to learn from being on this path? Thinking hard was making her brain tired. She took out the note included with the keys:

Along your journey, hold this pouch. Then use all the keys you find to unlock the potential of your mind.

She hoped she had the potential to do great things, but why did exploring her capabilities include going through a briar patch? She shivered. Retreat was the best option. Then, her eyes fell on one more sentence in small print at the bottom of the paper:

Repetition will help leave the past behind.

What did repetition have to do with potential? She had just repeated, "I can" and "I will." Did she need to repeat "courage"? And why? "Trust in what is trustworthy," her guide had said. It was worth a try. Stepping on a log, she called in a low voice, "Courage, courage, I have courage." Nothing changed. The thorns were still there. A little louder, she called, "Courage, courage, I have courage." Crockett barked. Now she was yelling, "Courage, courage, I have courage!" She could picture herself on a podium addressing hundreds of people – her people – motivating them to work on her ideas and creations. She yelled again, "I have the courage to do great things!"

Just then, from her elevated view, she saw a glimmer of light beyond the sea of thorny bushes. "Another gate, Crockett! We found it." As they passed the thorns, she took out the next key, "Confidence." She remembered what one of her favorite instructors in school had said, "Acts of courage bring confidence." Seeing herself in a position of leadership was rekindling her confidence. It could happen. Even though her arm was bleeding from the large scratch and she was exhausted, these distractions didn't need to stop her.

The gate easily swung open. Crockett pulled her toward the clearing ahead, which she gratefully affirmed by following quickly. There were no more thistles or thorns, and surrounding her were two beautiful meadows, one on each side of the path. She had to hold Crockett back as a family of bunnies crossed their path. Blooming flowers, hummingbirds, and even butterflies joined to create a blanket of color.

Catching her breath, she climbed on a rock to see it all. Before her was a scene not visible from the thorny patch. Because of the tall weeds and briars, she had little assurance of a change ahead. Was this clearing here to build her trust? The large gate in the distance had to hold the last key, "Joy." But before proceeding, she had one more thing to do. Yelling at the top of her lungs, she repeated phrases she hoped to remember, "I have confidence, and I am courageous. I am courageous!" "Joy" was a confusing word. It meant more than happiness because she could fake that feeling if needed. Was she feeling joy now, or was it the anticipation of her future possibilities bubbling up within her? A dependable friend who claimed she made it to her Summit had once told Mallery that she could have joy no matter what happened, even if she never made it to her Summit. Mallery wondered how that could be possible, as she had failed so many times.

She wanted to reach her Summit to find success. She would be tremendously disappointed if she didn't. Failure couldn't possibly produce feelings of joy. Yet something in her friends' words sparked a flicker of truth. Even though she had not yet reached her Summit, she did not feel like a failure. Instead, she felt elated.

"We'd better move, Crockett. We may be pitching our tent tonight." The "Joy" key fit perfectly, and the gate swung wide. Not one hundred feet ahead was a shack with a flickering light glowing through the shutters. The steps creaked, as she examined the weather-worn door up close. She knocked lightly, and it easily opened. A note on the table contained the message, "For MAL."

> Your silver pouch is now empty as you've discovered the keywords to help you enter the Cave of Discovery.

Crockett was paying no attention as he had already found a full dish of food by the door. All she knew about caves was that they were dark, damp, and cold. If a cave lay ahead, where was the mountain she was to climb? Cyber Hill had hardly been noticeable with all the gates and entrances and nothing like a mountain. Who knew what could be lurking inside a cave? Even though she longed to make a better life, her little town, Baybel, was not a cave. There was more:

> Don't be afraid. Remember, your guide will be close by. On this table is a small hand shovel and a map. Put the map in your silver pouch and the shovel in your backpack.

"A map! Crockett, a map." He kept eating. The Band of Hope tightened around her wrist. Still, the thought of journeying through a cave felt ominous. She read on:

> You have already used the key that will help you most, "Courage," but don't forget you have everything within you to continue your journey. Write about the courage you feel and your experience every day in your journal. The map has four places where you will uncover rare and valuable stones. Make sure you follow the path exactly and put each one in your bag. Tomorrow, you will enter the Cave of Discovery through the door in the back of this room.

That was it. The arched door in the back looked hand-hewn from a tree. She dared not open it now as it was pitch black outside. There was a healthy-sized bowl of soup with warm bread and fruit waiting at the table. She was famished but wrote a few words in her journal before eating:

> *How strange this day was – nothing normal at all. I've never lived my life expecting the unexpected. My schedule has followed a regular routine, day after day. Today was different. I repeated the words "I can"; "I will"; "I have courage;" and "I have confidence" several times. I'm not believing all those messages, but the anticipation of future possibilities is welling up within me. I think it could be joy.*

Crockett curled up on his bed by the fire and let out a dog-burp. She stifled a laugh as she eagerly ate every drop of soup. Then, she jotted down a few more thoughts:

> *Can I have joy if I don't make it to the Summit? I'd be more disappointed than joyful. But I want to live life encouraged by what I can accomplish, not discouraged about what I can't do.*

She could hardly believe that last phrase, but it was inspiring for her to reread it aloud. With that, she put her journal away and relaxed on the simple, comfortable cot in the corner. She focused on the sayings she so recently chanted, "I can; I can;" and "I will; I will." Courage and confidence welled up within her with the repetition. Then, she dropped into a deep sleep with dreams about rare and valuable stones awaiting her in the Cave of Discovery.

CHAPTER FIVE

The Gems of Opportunity

Mallery wondered how the hot bowl of oatmeal, juice, fresh fruit, and roll appeared on the table the next morning without her or Crockett hearing anyone enter the shack during the night. She wanted to ask her guide how food mysteriously appeared. They were most peculiar events. After putting the hand shovel in her backpack and the map in her silver pouch, she added the magically appearing snacks and sack lunch as well. With Crockett on his leash, she tentatively opened the back door, shivering at the burst of cool air. Stretching her leg until she felt the first deep step in the dimly lit cave, she had just enough light to see a path. However, she saw only shadows, no birds, bunnies, flowers, or meadow. Just rock, dirt, and shadows.

At the first meandering, she studied the map where a dotted line terminated at a large circle containing the number one. Next to it was the shape of a blue sapphire, which she assumed was the stone she was to uncover first. In a way, this process felt like the scavenger hunt games she and her friends played growing up. However, nothing of value had appeared on their lists, just everyday items like pillows, playing cards, and forks. Discovering real gems would be intriguing. She followed the beams of light coming through the crevices in the rocks until she came to the first spot on the map.

"Crockett, stop!" she shouted as her dog dragged her forward. He started biting the air around a small bush of azure flowers, blooming atop low, compact green branches. She swatted the air when a swarm of bees buzzed away from the bush. "I don't want to have to pull a stinger out of your nose! What were you thinking?" Crockett seemed not to hear her as he snapped at any movement.

She stooped to read the marker: "Omphalodes." They reminded her of the Forget-me-nots she cared for at home. Soft dirt surrounded the blue bush, so she used her shovel to dig right beside the marker. In a few moments, the metal hit a hard object. She uncovered the end of an oddly shaped chunk enclosed by what looked like a piece of hardened leather. This would be a joke on her if it was just a rock placed in a dirty bag. She lifted it out and eagerly untied the twine holding it together.

"Oh my!" She stared at the most beautiful blue stone she had ever seen, as velvety cobalt as the sky outside the cave. The square shape contained step cuts to make the multi-faceted gem sparkle with brilliance, even in the dim light. A paper fell out:

```
This blue sapphire signifies your rare, valuable skills.
As you look at it, realize you have unique abilities.
However, they are only valuable if you use them.
```

She immediately questioned how discovering keys and uncovering jewels could affirm her skills. Mallery hoped she had the potential to do great things. Unlocking those gates took trust, especially the one with the thistles. But this was even more bizarre. Was this jewel truly valuable? She had not felt valuable because she had stuffed her dreams behind the desk of her accountant job. What were her hidden skills? She'd helped one of her former bosses by sketching out an impressive plan for an office remodel. Their main office space consisted of a jumble of multiple-sized cubicles that blocked any natural light from entering the work area. Her plan replaced the cramped nooks with a spacious design, muted colors, and even streamlined cubicles that brightened the room. Mallery also suggested new wall coverings, flooring, and lighting to transform the space. When it was completed, productivity increased, and the boosted morale of the whole office brought her extreme satisfaction.

Even further, she had sketched out a detailed financial plan, which her boss followed. The whole project came in under budget and in less time than projected. This experience made her wonder if architectural design was a path she should take, yet it seemed too easy. Besides, she dreaded criticism from those who would see such a move as one of her "crazy ideas." She never took credit for the office plans. However, her boss did give her a nice bonus once the project was completed. She had taken "before and after" photos, too, placing them in her book of ideas, which gave her a sense of accomplishment. Since then, she had retreated from risk. At work, she stayed behind her computer, glued to her desk chair day after day. She dreamed of running her own business someday, but that seemed like a far-off dream.

She took out the map to determine her location and help her find the next gem. Doing the simple sketch on the map felt like what she did for the remodel, envisioning the plan from start to finish. It was like other plans she secretly stored in her book of ideas, uncomplicated, yet accurate.

In her journal, she wrote:

I found a beautiful sapphire. The note said it would affirm my rare and valuable skills, but I'm not sure how a stone can do that.

I'm fearful of expressing my ideas because I'm afraid to fail. But maybe some of my skills need to be uncovered, just like the stone. One of my unique, valuable skills may be in spatial reasoning. I can see plans from start to finish, all in my head.

Then she closed her book, speaking softly, "Courage, courage, I have courage." Her voice echoed from the cavern, "Courage, courage, I have courage." Her words sounded stronger. Mustering up more volume and intensity she yelled, "Courage, courage, I have courage!" The voice she heard grew in confidence and assurance.

She projected those words again, even louder, as there was no one to call her crazy. Visualizing images of her successful office design, she continued, "I have unique, valuable skills." But that was as far as she could construe as "Valuable skills, valuable skills" reverberated through the cavernous space. The band warmed her wrist as she put the stone and paper in her silver pouch and moved on. The map's dotted line wound to a large number two next to a picture of a ruby. After an hour of searching, she turned it upside down, wondering if she was reading the map correctly. With no offshoots from the main path, there was little chance she'd missed a turn. She didn't want to misread the directions, like the time she missed the start of a colleague's wedding when she misunderstood the out-of-town location, got lost, and drove to the wrong place. She recalculated and changed course, but the festivities were almost over when she arrived. Luckily, there was wedding cake left because she was famished after getting lost.

After an hour's search, bright red impatiens appeared. The blossoms grew right out of a rock. Soft soil surrounded them along with a plant label that looked just like her favorite popsicle stick – a clue. She started digging as fast as she could until she saw the edge of worn leather, darker than the previous find. Carefully lifting the mud-caked object, she pulled on the twine to unwrap the packet and gazed upon a magnificent heart-shaped ruby. Hearts reminded her of how she wished for a significant relationship. She once read a book that said fully loving someone else can only happen if a woman was secure in her own identity and worth. Feeling secure was a state that she hoped was within reach like her fortune in finding the stone. If she just kept these two stones, she'd be financially secure for a time, not disadvantaged. Even if the stones weren't valuable, she would look the part to stand tall and feel normal.

Lost in her thoughts, she almost forgot to read the paper enclosed, but the warm Band of Hope on her wrist brought her back to reality:

> This rare and valuable ruby signifies how rare and valuable you are. It also is a symbol of love.

She didn't feel rare and valuable and didn't want to be reminded that she had not yet found love, but she read on:

> After you discover your unique skills, combine them with what you love to do. That will create unlimited possibilities for an exciting and vibrant future that will inspire you and create a life of significance and meaning.

She wanted to believe it, but she felt uncomfortable in her own skin, especially at social events. She was boring and often at a loss for words. Unlike her, Treston was the fast-talking life of the party. The most attention he had ever paid her was when he didn't want her to go on this journey. Could it be that he didn't want her to do something he would never attempt? Maybe her family members felt threatened by what she could become. She took out her journal and recorded her thoughts:

> *I found a ruby, but it reminds me of how disappointed I am at not finding true love. I thought I'd have met the man of my dreams and settled down by now, but that hasn't happened. My closest*

companion is my dog. The note says to focus on what I love so I will try to do that. Even though I'm an accountant and that's brought me some success, I love design. I wake up thinking about layouts and transforming different spaces, taking them from where they are now to where they could be.

As she wrote, she felt the same joy she had experienced when writing about her office design and spatial reasoning. Yet she wondered how all this related to her Summit trip.

With the ruby safely secured in her silver pouch, she hoped it would help her find love. Gripping her bag, she sat back with Crockett to close her eyes for a brief catnap but then woke with a start, wondering how long she had slept. Two more stones remained. An amethyst was by the number three on the map. What would it be like to hold the purple gem? All she had was a fake amethyst necklace she had received for her birthday. The colored stone was so small it was hard to distinguish. She wore it anyway as it was a gift from a boy she dated for a time. She wondered if this next stone would be as valuable as the others.

As slivers of afternoon light shone through, Mallery followed the snakelike path leading to a vibrant purple plant, peonies that stood out against the drab grey and brown of the rocks and dirt. This had to be the spot, as she and her dog made the tricky navigation over a small rockslide obstructing their path.

"Crockett, slow down!" He kept forging ahead. After twenty minutes, she reached the tightly grouped peonies, a vibrant sight, especially in a cave. Then realizing Crockett must be thirsty, she set a small bowl down and emptied the remains of her water bottle in it.

"There must be magic in this cave, Crockett. How else could these plants live without a water source?" He kept drinking. Kneeling and digging, Mallery's shovel hit something solid but deeper than the other stones. It took ten minutes to unearth the leather-wrapped object, but when she finally had it in her hand, she clutched it tightly. She held up her birthstone, quite a sight to behold. She had never seen an amethyst of this rectangular size and brilliance. It looked real. In a strange way, it felt like the stone was part of her. It would be spectacular in a ring setting. The paper that fell out with the stone read:

Purple is a color of royalty. Your experience will give you additional status and power as you use your unique skills.

That didn't make sense. She stayed quiet behind her desk, working diligently not to draw attention to herself or her work. It was better that way. Her boss had given her quite a bit of extra work through the years as she was able to handle it thoroughly and quickly. In fact, that's how she had saved for this trip as she managed some very large projects on the side, none of which any of her co-workers recognized. She read on:

Think through all the areas of your experience as you will waste nothing. You will find ways to connect your experience with your skills and what you truly love to do. This combination will create multiple ideas and possibilities for your future.

There it was again, that phrase "what you truly love to do." It seemed like a far-off dream. But that's why making it to her Summit would help her. She could handle multiple projects and earn extra income. But could she make it in the area she loved? She had to record those thoughts:

I love handling large projects and detailed work, but does that make me good enough to pursue what I really want to do? I have always wondered what else I need to do to feel like I can compete, can keep up and can be as good as those who seem to have it all together. I wonder if they ever felt like I do, afraid to fail?

Closing her journal, she knew darkness would come all too soon, and this cave was dark enough in the day. However, she had to find the last stone before nightfall.

Mallery had been so preoccupied with the amethyst that she had lost track of time and realized a full hour had passed. She saw a large fern ahead, highlighted dramatically against a silver rock. Ferns grew in extremely shady places so finding one wasn't a surprise. Ferns reminded her of her mother, who could grow plants in any space. Mallery hadn't inherited her mother's green thumb. Plants she tried to grow in her small apartment died. When she got to the fern's label stick, it said, "Cinnamon Fern."

This was one of the hardiest ferns that could grow in complete shade. By the number four on the map was the word, "emerald." The only emerald she had seen belonged to Tamma, who wore her emerald necklace and matching earrings to show off her flawless complexion. Once again, she dug at the foot of the leafy plant. Because the fern was larger than the other plants, she kept hitting its spreading roots. Crockett started digging, too, throwing out huge clumps that completely covered Mallery in dirt.

She could hardly get the words out to stop him as she had to spit out a piece of root he had unearthed. The wide hole revealed an edge of the leather-wrapped gem. This spurred her to keep digging, and after several minutes, she uncovered the bundle that held a magnificent pear-shaped stone. Its brilliance took her breath away. She felt she could conquer the world by possessing a stone as fine as this emerald. Why was she the one to find them? Enclosed with the emerald was the message:

Finding this green emerald should inspire you to keep going and never quit. You will need patience and perseverance in the days ahead, but you have everything within you to keep going.

How much more patience and perseverance would it take? She'd already gone through the forest and stepped over and around thorns and thistles:

```
The secret is to keep growing and learning. If you have
that mindset, you will make it to your Summit. Defining
your skills, experience, and what you love to do is a
great start. Never, never quit. You will make it!
```

These notes spoke to her. Were they from her guide? She suddenly wondered where he was and where she was going to stay the night. She placed the large green teardrop in her silver pouch, along with the accompanying slip of paper. The pouch bulged with gems. She felt a bit richer and more confident of the journey ahead. She also took a large piece of the fern as a reminder of her mother. She knew it wouldn't stay green the whole trip, but she hoped to give it to her mom when returning home, a proof of her adventure.

She wanted to keep the stones as a valuable addition to her financial portfolio to make up for the time she had taken off work. That prospect excited her as she set off to discover a flat space to pitch her tent. She squeezed between two large boulders. Just beyond the rocks was a shed that looked more like a lean-to. On the edge was a sheer drop-off. Would it be safe for her to enter the shelter, much less stay the night? She approached it tentatively. Fortunately, the sturdy door at the entrance revealed a foundation that looked solid. The room held a familiar welcome but also a surprise.

Crockett's chomping on a bowl of food brought her attention to the room before her, where a steaming bowl of stew, bread, and fresh fruit sat on the table. Eating calmed her as she had a resting place. She saw some familiar pictures on the walls. Craven's image looked right at her from a simple, splintered frame. She shuddered as his eyes followed her eerily around the room. Shamere's picture hung in the frame beside Craven, looking a little askew through cracked glass. How appropriate as they both did so much together with fear and doubt as their guides. But neither of them would have ever come to this place alone, so their appearance here was a mystery.

Cagney's picture was across the room. Even though Mallery tried to look positively at her situation, her sister's name confirmed exactly what she was feeling at the moment, trapped in a lean-to placed precariously close to a cliff's edge. Treston and Tamma were both pictured on the other wall in ornately gilded frames. They got along well. She could almost hear them whispering, boasting about themselves, telling of their accomplishments. Just seeing their faces made her feel insignificant. The remaining picture made her feel a well of emotion. Her mother's eyes looked at her with kindness and support through the simple, small frame. They hadn't spoken much in past years, but she suddenly longed to see her, give her the fern, and hear her comforting voice. Even though their relationship had been strained, she still wanted her mother's affirmation. A well-cushioned cot stood in the corner with a beautiful quilt, but how was she to sleep with all these eyes looking on?

When she took out her journal, she noticed Craven was no longer looking at her. Her mother was gazing away, and no imagined whispers were coming from Treston or Tamma. She wrote her thoughts:

I am in a place where I felt so many eyes were on me when I walked in the door, but I wonder if that was just my imagination. I have hesitated pursuing so many of my plans and dreams because I felt others were looking at me with criticism, talking behind my back, and I could never measure up to their standards. Maybe that's what I'm supposed to learn here. It doesn't matter what others think, even if they are looking at me. I don't need their affirmation, though I'd still like to prove I can make it. I know I'm skilled in putting plans together, seeing the big picture. And I love design. I think I will start pursuing more training to be much better at what I know I can do and love to do.

Closing her journal, she collapsed on the cot. A deep sleep enveloped her. The next time she opened her eyes, a beam of light was coming through the cracked window. She had to get her bearings since she was still in a cave, facing a huge cliff just outside. The Band of Hope had grown tighter around her wrist. With no other map or instructions for the day ahead, she wondered what hope she really had.

Once again, a nutritious breakfast of steaming oatmeal, berries, a roll, and fresh juice awaited her. She didn't question how it got there, but it was remarkable. Still elated about the gemstones, Mallery felt the silver pouch in her backpack and gazed at the glistening contents inside. With more light, she saw the shack had a clean shower in the opposite corner, and it provided plenty of hot water, so welcoming after Crockett's digging had thrown dirt all over her the day before. She could barely turn around in the space but feeling the warmth and refreshment of the water invigorated her to quickly get on her way. She wrote:

If all else fails, I still have the gems. I'm actually torn. On one hand, I could go home now and be okay. I've gotten far enough to know where I want to go and what I want to do. But I still want to make it to my Summit to see where it will take me. There must be more.

Before leaving, Mallery took the photo of her mother off the wall. No one else would have any use for it, and it gave her comfort to carry a piece of home with her. She noticed a brief hand-written inscription on the back but didn't bother to read it. She carefully stepped out the front door. This was not a day for any missteps. She felt energized as she inhaled the invigorating cool air. The narrow path beyond the shack followed the cliff's edge. It was smooth and wide enough for her and Crockett.

Careful of her footing and holding Crockett close on his leash, she marveled at the beauty of the rock formations as she moved along the path. Filtered light flowed in with luminous designs dancing on the craggy rocks. Looking across the large chasm, she longed to know what was on the other side. She could see a meadow with a magnificent carpet of green grass and a flicker of butterfly wings. It would be perfect if a bridge could take her there.

After some time, she saw a lookout area, a welcome break from her careful maneuvering as her shoulders were stiff from concentrating on the path. Thankfully, the obedience training she had given Crockett stuck, and he stayed put, even laying down for a brief nap. She gingerly made her way to the cliff's edge to examine a small metal box that caught her eye. It was covered with rust and dirt, but a tiny ray of blue light radiated from the interior. She tried to move it, but it wouldn't budge an inch, firmly fixed against a large rock. She then tried in vain to open the latch. Though she wanted to move on, the light in the box made her long to discover its secret. Just like the keys, maybe the box would open a new opportunity for her. There must be some reason it was left in the middle of a cave. Not everything made sense right away, like the food and shelter she found each night. But she now realized the provision signified she was on the right path.

The illuminated hole was large enough to insert a multi-faceted object. She had no tools that would fit such an opening, only her hand shovel. Crockett was still resting calmly so this would buy her a little time to think, as her curiosity was piqued. Was there a secret hidden in this box? Maybe a map, more keys, or more jewels? She'd love more jewels. To retrieve her shovel in her backpack, she first took out the photo of her mother. She read the inscription on the back in her mother's handwriting: *I have always believed that you had everything within you to be successful. You now possess the gems that will help you unlock even more of your future.*

She wondered why her mother would mention gems. Their family had never owned anything of value, and her mom couldn't possibly know about the stones she'd found. While growing up, her mom was constantly correcting and scolding, never believing in her daughter. But as Mallery got older, their relationship was gradually changing. Even though still critical, deep down her mother did love her and wanted the best for her, judging by the note she read. Maybe "possess the gems" was a phrase her mother used. Anyway, how would her possession of the gems help her now with a rusty old box? Plus, Mallery counted on keeping the gems after her climb. In her opinion, "Finders, Keepers."

She kneeled to look at the metal box opening. It was square with one side arching up slightly, like a step cut for a gem. A startling thought hit her: Would this be for one of her gems? Why would she place a special gem in an old rusty box? And they were *her* gems, part of her security and success for an uncertain future. Would that success feeling disappear if she had to use one to open a box? She noticed the sapphire was closest to the shape of the box latch. She reread the paper attached to the sapphire:

```
This blue sapphire signifies your rare, valuable skills.
As you look at it, realize you have unique skills.
However, they are only valuable if you use them.
```

She carefully took out the magnificent square sapphire, holding it up to see the blue beam of light bounce off the artfully crafted cuts. Strangely, it seemed to match the box opening perfectly. As she touched the box, it felt warm. Was there some sort of life beneath the cold metal? Her mind started racing as she recalled her mother's words, *You now possess the gems that will help you unlock even more of your future.* But losing even one stone pained her. What if nothing happened? The box would still hold its secret inside. What if inserting the stone opened the box to reveal some creature that would jump out at her? She shivered. But then, what if there were more treasures inside? She had to find out.

Mallery carefully placed the sapphire in the opening and immediately the box latch released, startling her and Crockett, as he awoke from his brief nap with a yelp. She cautiously peered inside, disappointed that there were no more jewels. She spotted papers tightly rolled together with string. They seemed much larger than would fit in the small area. Unfolding them, she realized before her were a full set of plans, blueprints for a bridge.

CHAPTER SIX

The Bridge of Possibility

Suddenly, Mallery laughed out loud, her voice echoing through the cavern. She questioned the logic of plans for a bridge in a cave. With no supplies, she was by herself, and the chasm between her and the other side looked truly daunting. She could hardly trust herself and Crockett to stay safely on the path before them, much less think about walking across a bridge that may only be partially completed. However, she looked closely at the plans, as they did interest her. One of the papers held a birds-eye view, revealing a map. Another lookout area farther up the path was noted with a square, showing an existing drawbridge there.

A drawbridge would solve her dilemma of getting to the other side. Why would she need blueprints if the drawbridge was already in place? Looking more closely, she saw unfinished areas. She'd need to see the drawbridge for herself. Even if the drawbridge was long enough, would it work? A voice from behind her made her jump up. "Oh, you startled me!"

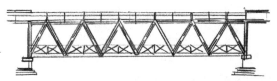

"Careful, Mallery!" Her guide replied. She gathered the pages that had flown out of her hands. Before she could formulate her questions, her guide continued, "You're right on schedule with your route. Do you need anything?"

"Oh, everything has been great, the places to stay, the food. But what am I supposed to do with these plans?" She had decided not to bring up the jewels though she realized he probably knew about them.

"You will need to do some work along the way."

"There is a drawbridge on the plans, correct? What will I need to do?"

"You'll need to finish it and will get further instructions and materials as you proceed." Mallery stood speechless. Her guide could tell she did not want to hear such news. "Mallery, you have the ability to complete the drawbridge."

"I have never done anything remotely like this. The plans look fascinating, but building? I'm all by myself. I can't."

"Really, you *can't*?"

Mallery hesitated, remembering the first key. "So you think that I *can* do this? By myself?"

"You have Crockett to help, don't you?" Her guide reached down to stroke the dog's head.

"Ha! Yes, Crockett is a huge help!"

"I believe in you. Everyone's journey is different. This task is part of yours." Mallery's thoughts immediately turned to the jewels, but she hesitated. "You will need this." He brought out a long, slender drafting pencil. "Use it to finish the blueprints."

The pencil looked like ones she had used at work, but much longer. Then her guide took out one more item: a book with a bright blue cover. "You should study the first chapter before doing anything else. You will then be ready to move on."

Mallery could not remember when she had last read a physical book, maybe during her school days. Listening to or watching programs was more convenient. Reading seemed old-fashioned now. Yet her dampened spirits, brought on by the dark, dank cave, melted away as she opened the book:

```
Importance of Weight and Balance, Best Materials,
Reasons for Failure, Regular Maintenance.
```

The first few pages grabbed her attention. When she looked up to comment, her guide had already gone. She couldn't see how this book was all she needed, along with a pencil and plans. She hoped her guide was mistaken. Perhaps she would find the drawbridge already completed. With Crockett settled beside her, she read the first chapter on weight and balance, which made sense in relation to bridge construction. If the bridge was not balanced correctly, it could tip or give way with pressure, as it would be unstable. Then her mind wandered to her most recent relationship, which was in many ways unstable. It felt like she was chasing the guy more than he was pursuing her. Sometimes, she'd change her evening plans to wait for his calls that wouldn't come. Other times, he'd call out of the blue, and they'd go to a party where she'd barely see him as he talked with his other friends until late.

When she saw him having lunch with a pretty colleague from the office down the street, she realized hers was a relationship of convenience. He called her whenever he needed a quick date. During that lunch he enjoyed with someone else, he looked at the woman and took her arm at the elbow in the way she always wished he would do for her. In that moment, she realized that theirs wasn't a relationship at all, just her wishful thinking. Would she ever have anyone who would be attracted to her for herself? She hoped that Mr. Right would show up someday.

The book showed many types of bridges. Studying the designs, she wondered what type of bridge would work best in this place. Since no foundation existed for a separate support in the middle of the chasm, she realized a truss design with its large group of triangles would be the best option. She was again pleasantly surprised how all the designs seemed to make sense to her. The thought energized her with a feeling of fulfillment. She unrolled the plans and noted the uncompleted areas. Before making her first mark, she noticed a ruler guide on the side of her pencil. This drafting pencil with measurement markings would aid in the exactness of her plan. There was no room for error in creating a bridge, but even if she could remember the principles, the math classes she took long ago wouldn't apply at all to the computations necessary for a bridge. Over and over, she calculated the number of triangular sections the bridge would need according to the plans in front of her. One error would be her downfall. The whole concept still seemed impossible.

She'd have to trust that the plan's dimensions were to scale as to the exact distance to the other side. Trust. There was that word again. Just trusting her guide for a journey to her Summit was a huge step. Now she had to trust in plans she found in a rusted metal box. She ate her lunch while she calculated the number of supports required to hold the weight. She remembered what she had written after finding the sapphire:

One of my unique, valuable skills may be in spatial reasoning. I can see plans from start to finish, all in my head.

Those words rang true as she visualized the complete project. Even though the plans were incomplete and fragmented, she finished easily and quickly. It looked good on paper; the design was beautiful. But the thought of walking across a structure that she was responsible for seemed daunting. Were her calculations correct? Would it hold her weight? She couldn't think of falling into the chasm or even worse, having Crockett go down with her. Looking at the book once more, she saw another highlighted phrase:

The intricate balance of a bridge is possible because of
equally weighted sections that hold up under pressure.

Pressure. That's what she was feeling. Stuck on the wrong side of a vast chasm, she was looking for a way across. So many areas of her life brought stress and pressure. She knew some of her issues were self-induced. She drove herself not only to measure up to a supposed objective at work but also in life. She often felt afraid to take a break from her responsibilities. Comparing her work with others didn't help. Even though her performance was just as good or better, she never felt like it was good enough. Taking out her journal, she wrote:

Part of the intricate balance of life is adding in sections of equal weight that will hold up under pressure. If I can identify what parts of my life are carrying extra weight, maybe I can balance them more easily not to feel like I'll collapse with exhaustion, stress, or discouragement.

She let that brilliant thought sink in. Moving forward, she noted the next lookout area. It didn't look too far on the map but looks were deceiving. Still, she briefly peeked at the next chapter on **"Best Materials"** before moving on:

```
Carefully choose materials after anticipating the force
of the load.
```

She knew about spending company money on materials for the office project design. She used the best materials within a reasonable budget. But building a bridge was different. The type and quality of materials used could make the difference in the structure supporting weight or completely collapsing under it. Her own weight would be the heaviest load, and cement or steel would be the best options and would hold her. However, assembling those materials seemed unobtainable. Trust, there it was again.

She rolled up the plans, gathered her belongings, and walked on the path. The other side of the chasm looked inviting as she and

Crockett walked close to the cliff's edge. The vibrant, dark green carpet of grass brilliantly reflected by what lay beyond, a bright light. Perhaps no one spoke of their actual journey to the Summit because the details seemed unbelievable – the chaotic forest, the garden, a cyber hill with the keys, the jewels, and plans for a bridge. According to her guide, everyone's journey was different, but details could still be beyond the scope of belief. Others would believe she'd gone completely mad if she told them too many details about her trip. She hoped to ask her guide her growing questions. Those thoughts kept her mind occupied for a full hour until she arrived at a large, primitive door built into a rock. Right next to the door stood a small, rusty box, indicated by the square on the plans, like the first one she had found. She sat on a flat rock, unrolled the plans, and took out her book. Nothing resembled the drawbridge in front of her. Was this all a joke?

"I feel foolish, Crockett." He cocked his head a little. "I know you don't understand, but here we are, stuck. I've finished designing a bridge of impossibility. How embarrassing!"

She didn't want to call for her guide, at least not yet. Reading more on the best materials was interesting, but interesting wouldn't get her across the cavern. With no drawbridge, her ability to use concrete or steel seemed out of the question. Still, it was fascinating to understand their use in design. For new construction sites in Baybel, when walking by work areas, she often lingered, studying the design process. Suddenly her gaze returned to the metal box by the door. Its distinct opening was also illuminated from an inner red light. The hole was shaped like a heart that reminded her, once again, of her longing for a significant relationship. The beautiful ruby was shaped like a heart. She whined, "No!" Crockett barked as if he agreed. She had wanted to keep it for a necklace to show off when she returned, pretending it was from someone special. No one would know the truth. Why give it up? She had the book, the pencil, and the plans.

The box was firmly attached to the door in the rock, but it had no handle. Would opening this box hold the secret to the door? Access to each night's lodging had not cost her anything so far. The book wasn't going to give her any clue to solving the puzzle of the box. It didn't seem fair to give up something of value with no guarantee of return. However, if the ruby would obtain something more fulfilling, then she could relinquish it though it felt like gambling, despite the fact she rarely even won card games.

Taking out her pouch, she withdrew the heart-shaped stone, held it in her palm, then ran her fingers over its grooves. She drew it to her chest, thinking of its necklace possibilities, pretending it meant a sign of love. The cool stone grew warm as she held it. She took out the paper included with the gem and read it aloud:

> This rare and valuable ruby signifies how rare and valuable you are. It also is a symbol of love. After you discover your unique skills, combine them with what you love to do. That will create unlimited possibilities for an exciting and vibrant future to inspire you and create a life of significance and meaning.

She echoed the phrase, "Life of significance, life of significance." Unlimited possibilities? Rare and valuable skills? What she loved to do? Her sketches on the plans for the bridge were accurate. She knew that. Yet no one she knew had such an ability. She re-read the note from her mother: *I have always believed that you had everything within you to be successful. You now possess the gems that will help you unlock even more of your future.* The ruby was meant to unlock the box and maybe open the door.

When she inserted the heart-shaped stone in the opening, the lid sprang open with a startling clang. The door in the rock tipped forward from the top about a foot, revealing a steel lever. As she pulled the lever, the door slowly lowered, extending into the chasm, like a drawbridge, but not far into the ravine. Directly behind the drawbridge, another door held a sign that read, "Welcome." The handle turned easily. Inside the room, Mallery spied a table with a steaming bowl of soup. A fireplace with flames leaped from the hot embers. The little haven built into the rock offered a welcome, warm reprieve after a day of watching every step on the path at the cliff's edge. Constantly reining in Crockett had been exhausting, too. Plus, it was painful to give up the brilliant ruby. She wrote:

> *I have had to give up another rare, treasured jewel today. I was reminded I have rare and treasured skills as well, but that didn't make me feel any better about relinquishing the stone.*

She took her time eating the hot meal and once again looked at the chapter on **"Best Materials"** while reveling in her warm surroundings. If she was to assemble a bridge with a truss design, she would need steel. She wondered how she could accomplish such a large project all by herself with no materials. The cot in the corner looked inviting because she was tired of thinking, studying, and drawing the impossible. Crockett had already eaten and was curled up, fast asleep. She added more thoughts in her journal:

> *My plans are good and possible, but I can't imagine how I will get the right materials to execute them. Even if I had materials, how can I put them together by myself?*

She put her journal down with a sigh and soon fell into a deep but restless sleep. Images of sapphires and rubies danced through her dreams all night.

CHAPTER SEVEN

The Reluctant Hero

Her room and the cave were so dark that she wasn't sure of the time when she awoke. As her eyes adjusted, she noticed objects in the growing light that she had not seen the night before. The walls that looked like rock she now saw were made of dark, rusted steel. Putting her hand on the surface, a vertical piece snapped off easily. Now she could see more pieces but hesitated, wondering if removing them would cause the entire structure to cave in on her. Pulling out the plans, she squinted to see another detail unnoticed previously. Numbers in faded print appeared along her detailed sketch, indicating independent pieces clipped together. Had those numbers just materialized overnight or was the lighting now showing what was once invisible? This had to be some clue, but to attach any of these pieces, would mean crawling to the end of the drawbridge.

The thought unnerved her. With her measuring pencil, she found the wall piece was the exact size as the triangular component in the plans.

The Band of Hope, almost forgotten, tightened around her wrist. She cautiously removed another wall plank, and sighed in relief when the room didn't fall in. The band tightened further. She was on the right track, especially as she noticed other pieces lining the walls. Mallery wanted to leave the dwelling that very moment to see how she could attach the pieces, but Crockett was sniffing his food that sat in a bag up on the table. She stopped to feed him and fed herself, too, hoping the yogurt, nuts, granola, juice, and roll would provide the energy she'd need. All tools went into her backpack, including the lunch and snacks. Then, she wrote in her journal:

I thought there was no hope, but I was wrong. There is a possibility that I can assemble the bridge myself if there are enough materials and I can manage with no help. Then I can cross to the other side, getting out of this dark place. The magic here is the only way I can explain how the materials appeared and were assembled with such accuracy. But I'm still wondering what I'm supposed to learn from giving up the beautiful ruby as I can't stop thinking about it.

"Crockett, be a good boy and stay right here. I'll be back." She gave him a hug and the rest of her breakfast roll. Picking up the two steel pieces, she went to view the drawbridge that was hardly a bridge at all – only some wood hanging over the chasm. Was it old? Was it rotted? Self-help books explained that one must "face the darkness and the unknown to realize new opportunities," but she didn't like that idea. On her hands and knees, she took one piece of steel in each hand, her safest approach. She inched forward slowly, dragging the steel, as she crawled tentatively to the right edge of the drawbridge, trying not to amass splinters in her knees. The wood shifted slightly under her weight. Adrenaline rushed through her body as she steadied herself. A gust of cold air came at her from the dark expanse.

"Breathe in. Breathe out." She wanted the endorphins, not the dizziness. Her brother had lectured her about the euphoria that endorphins bring when under stress, but she wasn't sure how accurate he was. As she inched forward, she saw where to connect the piece of metal. She reached over the side for the connection, which felt like locking in a piece of a life-sized jigsaw puzzle hanging from the edge of a roof down to the floor below. It snapped in place with a magnetic firmness.

"Breathe in. Breathe out." Mallery shifted her weight, creeping slowly to the other side of the drawbridge. The wood again swayed, but she was mentally ready and ignored any thought that could stop her. The next piece snapped in place, and even though relieved, she felt overwhelmed thinking of the task ahead to finish a bridge of this size. Then, the reverberation of a release echoed throughout the cave, not that different from the sound she heard after inserting the ruby in the metal box, though much louder. Metal vertical levers emerged from the newly connected pieces, each stamped with an arrow. Would those levers release some sort of trap door? Maybe this was a trick or maybe she was supposed to pull them, just like the one for the drawbridge. Indecision would not get her across. She grabbed the metal lever closest to her and tentatively pulled while holding her breath. A narrow steel beam moved with a jolt and extended from beneath the drawbridge all the way to the other side! She wondered how she'd explain the strange development to anyone. She had pulled this lever, and nothing bad happened but she'd also need to pull the other one. Moving more quickly, she crawled to the other side and confidently grabbed the next lever. But she did not get a good grip. It slipped out of her sweaty hand, and she lost her balance. Her scream echoed through the cavern, and she heard Crockett's barking from inside the shed.

At the last second, she grabbed the metal lever with her other hand and hung precariously over the edge, her feet dangling free. Was this going to be how it ended? Hanging off the side of a bridge? "Breathe in.

Breathe out." Dangling there felt like much of her life, as she'd barely hung on to her dreams. Why work so hard? And for what? Voices in her head shouted, "Mallery, Mallery, you're so ill-fated! Even your name is understated." She thought, *Maybe I should just give up.*

She needed to decide – fast. Her arms were throbbing, and Crockett's barking grew louder with mournful whines. She couldn't leave him, so she mustered all her energy, willing herself to get one leg on the drawbridge. Her body followed as she flopped down on the rough wood. "Breathe in. Breathe out." A large scrape on her arm bled onto her left sleeve. Crockett's barks turned to relentless whimpers.

"I'm okay Crockett! I'll be there soon!" She couldn't wait to curl up next to him and sleep the rest of the day, but for now, she lay still on the bridge, steadying herself. Building a bridge wasn't what she imagined in her climb to the Summit. Wasn't the journey supposed to be inspirational and fulfilling? This task was hard and harrowing. However, now was not the time to give up. She needed to get over the chasm. Mallery did not want to not empower Shamere, Cagney, and others by giving in to their negative messages, predictions, accusations, and pessimism. This experience would take not only physical exertion but also mental fortitude.

To reach the other side could give her enough courage, along with the jewels, to return home.

Then she noticed that the second lever had lowered while she was falling, extending the other narrow steel beam across the cavern. She sighed in relief and a wave of thankfulness. Now, should she crawl across those narrow beams? The answer was obvious. She had to finish the job to make a way for Crockett to cross. The truss bridge would be a much safer choice than relying on the slim extensions. If the materials were available, she had to finish the project. Now Crockett was yelping and crying.

"I'm coming, boy!" She ran to open the door and gave her traveling companion a one-armed hug. "Good boy."

With a first aid kit, she cleaned up the scrape on her arm, thankful it was the only consequence of losing her balance. Then, taking two more pieces of steel off the walls, she looked at her plans to confirm their placement.

"I'll be back, Crockett." Though he looked at her with sad puppy-dog eyes, she ventured out again to the drawbridge. When she hesitated, the vision of nearly falling off the bridge replayed in slow motion. Suddenly, a shadowy figure moved toward her. She looked for her guide, but then her heart sank. Beeshman, an old but disliked acquaintance, stood before her, his veiny biceps bulging from his tight tank top.

"Beeshman, what are you doing here?" She wanted to run and hide. How he had gotten through all the gates and dense forest, especially as he was underdressed for the cold cavern?

"I can't believe you came out here when I explained it was a waste of time!" His deep voice echoed through the cavern, "Waste of time, waste of time."

Mallery's tongue stuck to the roof of her mouth. It didn't seem fair having to face him after all she had just been through.

"You can't make it across the cavern! In fact, your screams are still echoing all the way to the entrance. If you fell, you and your dog, you'd *both* die!"

His words, "You'd both die, you'd both die," echoed through the darkness. Mallery closed her eyes, "Breathe in. Breathe out." Then she looked him straight in the eye, "I will get to the other side!"

"You're kidding yourself. Besides, the other side only *looks* better. It really holds misery and failure. I know." His bulging eyes and round face atop his trim body made him look like a bouncy bobblehead doll. Mallery clenched her fists. Who was he to discourage her?

With a surprising burst of confidence, Mallery shouted, "I can build this bridge!" Crockett barked insistently, and she wished he was by her side.

"No way! It won't hold you. You'll see," Beeshman laughed. "Look, your arm is still bleeding from your last failed try."

She yelled over Crockett's yelps, "The bridge will be strong enough. I calculated the weight and the dimensions. And Crockett, my good dog, will be right with me."

"Ha! Since when can you draw plans? You're no architect. You can barely do basic math. You're wasting your time, and those *jewels* won't save you either." His eyes were little slits now, looking like a creature crouched, waiting for the kill, "If you give me the jewels, I'll help you get back home."

How did he know about the jewels? He had not made it to his Summit and had discouraged her, telling her the journey was a waste of time. Now she was angry and wished he was an ant, so she could just step on him. He lunged forward, grabbing her wrist. With a scream and a turn, Mallery escaped his grasp, grabbed a metal bar, and hit his shins with all her might. "Get away from me. I will not quit!"

He fell to the ground. "I will not quit! I will not quit!" echoed through the cave. Crockett stopped barking, and stillness resounded from the cold surroundings, though the metal bar remained solidly anchored in her hand.

Beeshman backed off, scooting in an inverted backwards crawl, like a crab, scuttling away. His voice droned on in mumbled phrases about her never finishing the journey and losing everything. With every sentence, the timbre of his voice rose, making him sound like a cartoon character speaking through a helium balloon. Finally, he got to his feet, but tripped, still off balance while muttering warnings as he disappeared into the darkness.

Through her hot tears, Mallery smiled. She'd stood up for herself! The resolve she exercised with courage was new for her. Crockett, overjoyed, gave her dog-kisses. After a short rest, she hid her backpack in the room. Crockett would be standing guard, but his bark was worse than his bite. She didn't want to risk losing the two remaining jewels in case another character like Beeshman crossed her path. Embracing her resolve, she employed discipline and diligence to complete the bridge. The phrase, "To face the darkness and the unknown in order to realize any new opportunity," now made sense. She would finish reading that book when she returned. Deliberately, she climbed to the edge of the drawbridge. She attached horizontal bars across the extended long beams, creating a sturdy truss. She secured a small safety rope around her waist to avoid a tragic fall. When she returned to the room for lunch, Crockett ran circles around her like she had been gone for days.

"Calm down, boy!" She looked around, to check for intruders. "You have to be on your best behavior when we cross the bridge." She took out her lunch and then saw the paneling on the walls. This element had not been revealed until the steel was removed. Would those wood pieces fit as extra supports for the bridge? She couldn't wait to find out, even if the room fell in. After snapping one plank off easily, she left her lunch to crawl onto the bridge. The plank laid flat for a perfect fit. Finding those additional pieces was like the times she had discovered extra resources and finances for her clients. She enjoyed resolving difficult business projects. For once, she got to experience a positive design resolution for herself.

Now, she and Crockett would have a solid foundation. She spent the rest of the day assembling all the pieces on the bridge. To get Crockett across, though, she still wanted side rails. However, she had nothing to make them. She would have to be satisfied with the current design. Still, she felt proud of her magnificent project. She snapped a quick picture just to preserve the image of her work. She recalled her conversation with Beeshman and felt just as proud of it. She would double-check all areas of her work so they could cross the bridge the next day.

Caution reminded her to study the next chapter in the book **"Reasons for Failure."** She read while devouring the hot meal left on the table. She learned fascinating facts about different bridge failures. She didn't want to overlook anything. The main reasons for failure included a combination of issues, like structural design deficiencies, corrosion, or overloading. There would be no heavy traffic as only she and Crockett would be crossing it the next morning although she wondered what the future held for the bridge. Since it was fully built, would it last for others on the same journey or would someone destroy it to keep others from passing? She wouldn't put that past someone like Beeshman.

As far as structure, she had double and triple-checked each connection. Every steel beam she placed took her farther out of her comfort zone. The wood planks made the flooring fit tightly, but a side might come loose if not locked in its exact groove. With no side rails, Mallery would have to trust both her balance and the structure. After such a full day, she didn't have the energy to think deeply of anything but wrote her thoughts quickly in her journal:

Today I demonstrated courage, standing up to Beeshman. I want this bridge to work but feel that standing up to him was just as important, if not more. The bridge is done, and I am confident it will hold me on my journey to the other side though I will admit I'm a bit nervous about crossing without a rail for balance while walking and holding on to Crockett. I will need to walk as if there were rails, with courage and every bit of confidence I can possibly muster.

Her thoughts flowed quickly now:

I do wonder what causes failure and not just for a bridge. Does a person fail because she quits too soon or she doesn't assemble the right pieces for success? Beeshman seems so confident, but overconfidence could also be a reason why he never constructed a solid plan. Maybe that's why he never got to his Summit. If a person doesn't thoroughly account for his own weaknesses, he could experience failure in life, similar to the failure of a bridge if weaknesses aren't resolved. It pays to be introspective. I feel sorry for him, almost. I'm still annoyed that he tried to intimidate me to make me quit, even wanting me to hand over the jewels. His own inadequacies and failures held him back. He felt, by putting me down, he could lift his own status. It was a cheap shot, but he is the real loser.

Her eyes were now fluttering, so she put her pen down before it began blindly scribbling on its own. The bridge didn't need any more help – it was done. She was hoping to fall asleep quickly and her wish was granted as she could remember nothing more after that thought.

CHAPTER EIGHT

The Land of Allure

Mallery couldn't remember a time when she had slept so soundly. Though she knew her body was refreshed, a feeling of grogginess weighed her down. After a few moments, she realized where she was, so her disorientation faded. Today, she and Crockett would cross the large cavern outside her door. She packed her bag carefully, finished the light breakfast of berries, fruit, and yogurt that had appeared overnight and slipped her lunch bag in beside her journal. A note was on the table:

LAND OF ALLURE

THE IDEA FACTORY JUST AHEAD

CREATIVITY IS A WAY TO PROGRESS AND HAS NO LIMITS. STICKING WITH THE ORDINARY AND AVERAGE WILL KEEP YOU STUCK. THE UNINSPIRED AND ORDINARY ARE DESTINED FOR A LIFE OF MEDIOCRITY.

> Your time is your most valued possession. Stay on course and don't let any fabricated validation

distract you from your purpose. Just as a bridge needs
to be solidly built, so do segments in your life. Don't
let anything hinder you from your destination.

Nothing would hinder her now. She tucked the note in her bag. The land beyond the chasm looked as inviting as the day before. Glimmering light streamed through cracks in the overhead rocks, illuminating small sections of the bridge and accentuating their path of escape. Her elation made it hard to hold back. With her camera, she snapped more pictures of the bridge, highlighting the beauty of the destination ahead. A photo of the shack documented the dark place where she had begun this challenge.

Belief required action. She'd need to step out, trusting that the narrow pathway she had built would take her across the chasm safely. Even though assembled correctly, the real test was using the structure. She recorded her weighty thoughts:

Does a person fail because she quits too soon, or she doesn't assemble the right pieces for success? If a person never thoroughly accounts for her own weaknesses, she could experience failure in life, very similar to failure of a bridge if weaknesses aren't resolved.

She had done her homework, even checking for failure. The bridge would hold.

"Okay Crockett, we're going for it." She held his leash tightly, adjusted her backpack, and took her first step. The bridge held, but she felt a bit wobbly with no handrail. She closed her eyes and stood motionless to steady her balance and calm her breathing. She visualized rails to serve as her guide. She must keep her eyes on the goal, getting to the other side, one step, then another. Crockett stayed close to her, as she only had to pull on his leash once. She focused on a large, blossoming bush straight ahead and counted her steps: Ten, twenty, thirty, forty. Suddenly, she found herself on the other side. Her confidence soared with relief, victory, and liberating freedom.

"We made it!" Crockett, just as excited, jumped up to let her hold his front legs. She led him in a little dog-dance, until Crockett lost interest and his balance. "It's okay, Crockett. Good boy." She grabbed a doggy treat from her bag, and he gobbled it with a chomp. She felt elation just as she had after her office remodel plans had turned out successfully. She had kept her balance, both mentally and physically, not falling into Beeshman's trap. Seeing a beautiful green valley ahead instead of the cave's darkness lifted her spirits. Inhaling the fragrance, she saw the path to sunlight would be her way out. She quickened her pace and let Crockett off his leash so he could run circles around her. Her heart whirred in excitement along with him as he jumped and ran through the tall grass.

Another twenty minutes brought her to the mouth of the cave where its opening flooded light to warm her entire being. In the distance, she could see the faint outline of a town nestled against the hills, but no visible mountains. How much farther to her Summit? Her inner glow of hope starkly contrasted the cave's darkness. Crockett, back in his element, chased butterflies and grabbed at floating dandelion pollen. She skipped, too, which she hadn't done since she played hopscotch as a young girl, but the time was right to skip again.

Her brisk pace brought her upon a sign located by hut-like structures, but she could see no sign of activity ahead. The sign, printed in bold, finely crafted letters read, "Land of Allure: The Idea Factory just ahead." Under the title, faded text read: "Creativity is a way to progress and has no limits. Sticking with the ordinary and average will keep you stuck. The uninspired and ordinary are destined for a life of mediocrity."

Mediocrity. Many people working in her office just put in their time, waiting for the weekends. She didn't want to live the rest of her life contented with the mundane. So she'd have to set herself apart to be better than good enough. The pictures of her craftsmanship were a start in her breaking away from the ordinary and the average.

Advancing, she found the first building closed, but it looked fascinating. Peering inside the dirty windows, she spied tables filled with large, half-done sketches, multiple boxes with measuring instruments of varying sizes and colored papers and blocks in all configurations. Other workspaces and whiteboards held faded drawings. To her, it looked like a colorful preschool for adults and made her want to go inside and play. Wiping the dirt off the glass with her sleeve, she wondered what was created here. Some of the projects looked unfinished. A multicolored sign above the main door read, "The Idea Factory," but the space stood empty.

The next building featured another skillfully crafted sign, "Seminar Clone Factory." She could hear voices coming from inside where a group of people, all facing each other, repeated similar lines. They were imitating each other's phrases and voice quality. She had to look carefully to see whose mouth was moving as it was difficult to distinguish who was speaking. Even timbres and inflections of the voices were similar though not monotone. The monitors served as prompters that displayed the identical phrases.

She and Crockett walked through the open door. She saw signs labeled, "Event Planning" with speech titles listing Seminar 1: Voice Quality; Seminar 2: Messaging, and Seminar 3: Marketing. One person was labeling each section with a large, inked stamp that left an identical impression on each person's chart. The occupants wore similar dark blue blazers, had their hair pulled back, and exhibited calm mannerisms. She wondered if there was a Seminar for "Subject Matter" as she enjoyed inspirational and personable seminars. Did any of these people ever visit the Idea Factory? Although the people were hard at work, Mallery couldn't get anyone's attention. She decided to walk across the street where a smaller, less ornate sign said, "Styleless Music Shop."

The quaint interior had gold records lining the walls. The décor, eclectic and clean, featured signed photos accompanying many of the framed albums. Several rooms lined the sides, but the central studio area caught her attention. Slipping by the front counter, she quietly slid into the adjoining chamber. "Shh, Crocket," she whispered, holding tightly to his leash. The studio sound board spanned the length of the counter with multiple screens showing volume controls and sound waves. A busy engineer was intently editing one section. She stood quietly observing, thankful that Crockett had lain down at her feet. The young soloist in the soundproof booth, separated by a window from the controls, was earnestly crooning a series of "oohs" and "ahs" into the microphone. Lots of repetition with an emotive, breathless sound, the music resembled the choruses of several songs she had recently heard.

This sound, popular with some, lacked the complexity of other music. Since her mother had played many standard classics during her childhood, she understood how much variety and creativity in lyrics was possible. She loved intriguing melodic lines and harmonies that caught her ear. Not many current songs had caught her ear in that same way. She wondered if the Seminar Clone Factory and the Styleless Music Shop worked together. Did they reflect the "uninspired and ordinary" that were "destined for a life of mediocrity?"

She pulled Crockett up and slipped out the front entrance.

The next building bore a dilapidated sign, "Office of Public Service." Maybe here someone could give her information about this village. Inside the dank, neglected interior, the posted mission statement, torn on one side read, "Think tank for good-paying jobs." She wondered what strategy and research could possibly come out of such an uninspiring place. The surrounding walls contained signs for "Think Tank Jobs," listing several positions: Relationship Manager, Research Assistant, External Affairs, City Rescue Plan and Report Specialist. Another sign read, "What Are You Looking For?" followed by a numbered list: 1-Limited Hours? 2-Secure Tenure? 3-Lifetime Benefits? 4-Free Think Tank of Ideas? 5-Paid Vacation?

The lifetime benefits and tenure sounded desirable. This Think Tank seemed intriguing and innovative. Though from what she could see, the building held no creativity or workers of any kind. She loved

71

creating. To redesign this entire building to be brighter and more productive would be a challenge. Her stay would be short, but certainly they could use her skills even for a couple days. She returned to the main entrance, leaving the empty space behind. That's when she noticed a sign on the door: "Gone to the Social Media Circus." Now, that explained why so few people were around, even in the Idea Factory. The circus sounded wonderful. In her imagination, she was, once again, a child, fascinated with the clowns' antics, peculiar-looking performers, and most of all, the high-wire act with artists in sparkly costumes, doing impressive acrobatics. The flashing lights and calliope sounds had always mesmerized her.

A large arrow, outlined with bright colors glistening in the sun, pointed toward a hill just ahead. She and Crockett hurried up the sloped path toward the music and laughter. At the crest, the scene offered up a cacophony of sounds, a kaleidoscope of colors, and myriad of lights, along with sweet, pungent smells that blanketed the expanse. The area before her was so large that she couldn't see its end. The sweet aroma of funnel cakes, her favorite junk food, filled her nostrils, as Crockett feverishly sniffed the air. The clowns, animals, rides, and multiple booths all played their own version of the same song. Multiple tents, spaced a good distance apart, bordered a large roundabout in the center where tiny cars circled endlessly, stopping to pick up, then drop off clowns, performers, and spectators. Mallery couldn't recall ever seeing a roundabout in the middle of a circus, but it certainly made sense as this was a large area.

Obviously, the workers from the Idea Factory had been drawn to all the circus activity, colors, lights, and sounds. Like them, Mallery realized that work could have held her back, too. She would rather spend the day exploring, reveling in the stimulation surrounding her. People were flocking into the first big, blue-trimmed tent, bearing a huge sign that read, "FriendLand."

"C'mon Crockett!" She pulled on his leash toward the main entrance, where an electronic sign board featured rotating stories and posts: "We're in the 'Social Media Circus!'" The noise level in the blue tent contrasted starkly from her experiences thus far on her journey. The carnival-like surroundings revealed an area with bean bags labeled with emojis denoting responses, such as "like," "love," "sad," "thumbs up," "angry,' or "laughing." Behind the bags stood a large wooden board with round holes, with each hole containing point values of 5, 10, 20, and 50. By earning 100 points, participants could purchase "likes."

At another counter, a woman worked busily while a long line of people waited to see her. As Mallery drew closer, she saw written in small print: "Counseling Center for Unfriending: Completely Private." She pondered whether she should wait in this line now or later. How private was it? She had certain family members she wanted to "unfriend," but she feared the backlash of such an action. A completely confidential counseling session could prove helpful, especially upon her return. Eventually, she would have to confront her critical friends and relatives, those who crushed her dreams and mocked her social media posts. Standing up to Beeshman in that cave was one thing, but would she be that strong back home? She didn't know. She hoped to have courage enough to tell everyone about reaching her Summit. That is, if she made it.

At another counter, a large poster advertised a "Need Friends" seminar.

"What's your dog's name?" The stranger's question brought Mallery back to the present.

"Crockett." The young woman patted Crockett's head. Loving the attention, the dog rewarded her with a few licks.

"When's the seminar on friends?" Mallery inquired.

"It's over for today," the woman responded. "If you're interested, you can attend tomorrow. It repeats daily."

Mallery decided she would return the following day. She needed friends who shared her goal of getting to their Summit, even if they only associated online. At the side of the counter, a handy chute said,

"Personal Messages." She imagined writing a note that would be sucked up in a vacuum tube to go directly to a "friend." This feature made sense. For in the FriendLand tent, as a person increased her collection of friends, she could send them greetings immediately. Who would Mallery send messages to? That "Need Friends" seminar might help her find out. Her mind raced with the possibilities since she needed better contacts.

Maybe with those emoji bean bags, she could also gain some likes on her stories. She could add friends that way and send them all messages. What harm would there be in spending an extra day or two right here enjoying herself? Plus, Crockett relished the action and attention. Was it just this morning when she had crossed the bridge? That thought reminded her of the note she'd found:

> Just as a bridge needs to be solidly built, so do segments in your life. Don't let anything hinder you from getting to your destination.

This circus wasn't a hindrance. It couldn't be. Taking advantage of FriendLand's resources would only help her. Crockett's loud barking caused some blue birds to quickly fly out of a side entrance, tweeting noisily. She almost tripped over a loose bean bag, as he pulled her out into the open. The birds flew high, as Crockett ran after them, until they entered an adjacent tent. The chirping grew louder when she approached. With fluttering wings, clusters of birds perched high in an atrium. Crockett kept barking as if he understood their feathered language.

"What are they saying, Crockett?" In answer, he just kept barking. "Shh! Let's see what's in the main area." She pulled him over to a booth with a sign reading, "140-280 Characters that Will Get You Noticed." A nearby counter held free pamphlets entitled, "Increase Your Followers on 'BlueBird.'" Mallery took one. Coming up with pithy, clever sayings had never been easy for her. She wondered if her ideas would be better received with slick slogans attached. The pamphlet advertised "approved, customized phrases" for most any field. If she could increase her following using these aids, she wouldn't have to rely on her own ideas and creativity. That was tempting.

In the distance, another large tent shone with bright lights. She would have to enter the roundabout to reach it. Entrance to the roadway meant hailing down one of those tiny vehicles, but the whizzing cars were quickly snatched up by workers or costumed circus characters. Having Crockett made it more challenging. She'd need to move fast and deliberately. So she shoved forward and crowded in front of a thin man with a fat goatee. No signs indicated where to get on or off. Yet many of the vehicles stopped at the same place. If the clowns, animals, music makers, and others circling this roundabout could make it, surely, she could as well.

Surprisingly, Crockett helped because he jumped in the next car, pulling her quickly in behind him. Positioning herself behind the steering wheel, the car lurched forward, and that was when she discovered the vehicle had no steering mechanism or brakes. This self-driving car could circle until it decided her fate. "Breathe in. Breathe out." Crockett was crouched on the floorboard. She hoped he wouldn't be sick. While others were exiting, her car kept orbiting the roundabout. Then she heard the other drivers shouting their directions.

"Take me to the big white tent to the right," she called, but the car didn't respond. So she mustered more courage and said a little louder, "Take me to the big white tent to the right." Again, no response. Then in her most confident tone, she yelled, "Take me to the big white tent!" Her car pulled to the right, but then circled again. What was the secret? By now, more traffic crowded the lanes. A strong man with his huge barbell weight, accompanied by a bearded lady, aggressively cut in front of her, moving to the right as his car slowed down. She yelled one more time, "To the big white tent!" Amazingly, her vehicle followed the circus couple as they exited. As her car reduced speed, she hoped to get out unscathed and escape that couple. When her car stopped with a jolt, she and Crockett disembarked. Relieved, she walked away from that roundabout rollercoaster, thankful her legs held up as she gripped Crockett's leash and headed toward the well-lit tent.

Lights immediately flashed as she approached. Angled cameras high above rotated in the space. Some cameras looked like smart phones elevated on selfie sticks. She turned her head away to avoid impromptu photos displaying her face on the monitors. She wasn't polished and ready for a photo shoot after that cave drama. She could see other pictures, mostly selfie shots, along the entrance. This had to be Tinsel-cam, the app for photo and video sharing, perfect for a Social Media Circus.

Taking good photos had always been a challenge for her. Her shots fell short of other profiles that were uniform and beautiful, even color coordinated. Tamma had pictures down to a science. In contrast, Mallery's attempts to look relevant appeared silly and fake. Worse yet, she felt old, dumpy, and dated when she tried to look fashionable. Inside, the tent held stations for stylized hair and applied makeup with creative backdrops. In the makeup chair, a woman displayed her "before" photo with her "after" image. She did not look like the same person, for now she had a clear complexion, a crisp outfit, and a professional hair style. Even her double chin, prominent in the original photo, was disguised with a fashionable scarf. The sight of this transformation made Mallery long for her own makeover. What was so wrong with recreating her image? In a couple of days, she could enhance her profile and overall look. With these types of photos, she could tout her bridge-building skills with pictures that made her look smart as well as beautiful. She'd just have to work extra hard to live up to the image she created.

The Social Media Circus was quickly becoming the place she wanted to be. After all, the inscription on the sign at the entrance said, "Creativity is a way to progress and has no limits. Sticking with the ordinary and average will keep you stuck." The excitement and activity here felt inspiring and stimulating, though Crockett seemed bored, as he took a quick nap. However, creativity had its costs, especially to obtain the exceptional look she desired. She thought, then, of her jewels. Should she sell them? Perhaps she could a find a buyer for one. Then she'd be set.

After observing a few more photo sessions, which looked similar, she saw groups leaving as they mumbled something about a trapeze act. Her heart skipped a beat. She loved high wire acts. Even though she wasn't ready to leave Tinsel-cam, she soon had no choice as the surrounding booths closed one by one. Pushed by the crowd, she called out for a car on the roundabout and quickly got a vehicle. Confidently, she had pulled Crockett's leash to help get the car, as she cut in front of a sad-faced clown. When she passed, he honked his blue nose in protest. While the car circled, she spied a sign that said, "To the Summit." She felt a pang. Should she exit there?

Instead, Mallery moved ahead, not wanting to miss the circus action. She shouted the stop command, and the car responded. Elated, she and Crockett exited to join the crowds shoving into a gigantic white tent. Even though heights made Mallery's stomach turn, trapeze artists had always intrigued her. Their thin shapes and scant costumes glittered with each move. She pushed Crockett forward to help her find a seat, but it wasn't easy among the swarm gathered on bleachers. When the high wire acrobats leaped into the spotlight, Mallery imagined flying, her hair streaming as she twisted and turned, flexible as a plastic toy figure. With the wind on her face, she caught the outstretched arms of her handsome partner, who held her tightly as they dangled precariously from a thin bar. With every move, the crowd cheered loudly. She closed her eyes, lost in the moment. Then, suddenly, he let her hands go and her mind jolted back to reality as Crockett's cold, wet nose pushed against her leg.

Peering into the center circle, she saw the performers linked together by ropes with a web of nets below. Several of the acrobats had "like me" and "connect" written in bold blue letters on their costumes. "My Network" was written on many rows of seats in the arena. This had to be Connector, the social networking for business professionals. She sat up straighter, knowing important businesspeople would be in the audience. To help her career, she must locate the influential ones to add to her contacts. However, making the right connections would take time with so many possibilities. Perhaps, in this circus, she'd discover the intellectual stimulation she craved. It might just be the place to get unstuck. But she knew no one and hoped the isolation she felt would dissolve with the right relationships.

Meanwhile, the acrobats continued to soar, tumble, and dance in the center circle. Mallery felt torn between exploring more of the action or moving on to find dinner. She wished she hadn't seen that "To the Summit" sign on the roundabout. Yet staying was only a minor detour. Eventually she'd reach the Summit. With more to discover, she couldn't leave, at least not yet. When she reached into her bag, her hand fell on that morning's note:

Your time is your most valued possession. Stay on course and don't let any fabricated validation distract you from your purpose. Just as a bridge needs to be solidly built, so do segments in your life. Don't let anything hinder you from getting to your destination.

This life segment was important, for she was building it, piece by piece like the bridge. She shoved the note away and searched on her phone for a place to spend the night. The map directed her back to the Land of Allure, marking a spot inside the Idea Factory. She couldn't imagine it as a place to sleep with its lonely rooms and dusty windows. Thankful for Crockett's company, she followed the map away from the lights and excitement. It seemed a shame to retire early, but the setting sun left her no choice. The directions said to arrive at the factory before full darkness set in. Several "no vacancy" signs blinked on as she entered a vehicle on the roundabout. Speaking the directions loudly and clearly, the car responded easily, letting her off at the Land of Allure.

At the factory entrance, she could see a light burning. The sight lifted her spirits. She hoped for a quiet place to settle her thoughts. Even though she had felt perfectly safe alone in the cave, being here felt different. Images of clowns with garishly painted faces and carnival characters who appeared randomly in the streets provoked a sense of uncertainty. The atmosphere contrasted with the cave's dark surroundings. Its bright, energetic facade held the illusion of an exciting future. The front of the Idea Factory remained unoccupied and undisturbed, but the backroom door was unlocked, so she entered cautiously. Before her stood a table with a hot meal, just like other times. This sight further justified her decision to stay awhile at the circus. If she was supposed to exit at the Summit sign on the roundabout, a hot meal wouldn't be provided. Then she saw the note:

Please enjoy the hot meal. I will be there shortly.
Your guide.

Her guide would understand her desire to stay at least a week. Her reasons were all justified. Propping up her social media profiles and increasing her connections would only help her in Baybel. Behind the closed door, skillfully crafted signs hung on the walls bearing these messages:

Striving to conform creates limits.
Copying represses true potential.
Innovation leads to the extraordinary.

Despite these signs, no one worked in this building where dust lay on the tables and cobwebs hung in the corners. Crockett found his dish of food as her stomach growled. As she ate, she decided to attend the "Need Friends" seminar the next day. She could probably spend a day at each location. What would be the harm in spending two weeks here? While lost in her thoughts, her guide entered. She leapt out of her chair when he gently touched her shoulder.

"Oh, I didn't hear you come in! It's good to see you. I had such an interesting day that I want to stay here a while."

The guide gave Crockett a treat. "I knew you would find it tempting. This happens often when people enter the circus."

"Of course, I want to make it to my Summit. I'm not planning to quit. However, this place has potential to expand my networks and horizons. It feels right."

"But this circus is not the place to do it," he said.

Mallery's confusion showed on her face, and her shoulders stiffened. The silence was awkward. "But there is so much here…"

"Staying is a temporary fix. Remember, true friends and contacts do not disappear with a click."

Mallery winced at his response. This opportunity to create the perfect profile, to become an insider, she couldn't ignore. Besides, she deserved it after all her struggles and accomplishments.

"Status and power don't come from the ordinary, but the extraordinary," her guide explained. "You have unique abilities, and what you experienced today will not capitalize on those. Persistence will help you build your strengths to make you even stronger. Avoid shells that are easily broken. You must make your own decision, but take time to consider the consequences of staying, Mallery.

With that, her guide said goodbye. Her mind was racing. Consequences? What could be so wrong with staying? She deserved a break since she successfully built a bridge, stood up to Beeshman, and still had two jewels. Mallery looked around the room, observing the signs once more. She read them aloud:

Striving to conform creates limits.
Copying represses true potential.
Innovation leads to the extraordinary.

"The extraordinary." That's what she wanted, and her guide had told her this element brought authentic status and power. Right here, the Idea Factory offered innovation and creativity. Then a sobering thought struck. Did people get stuck here and never finish climbing their Summit?

She didn't want to be stuck. She took out her journal to write before making her final decision, but knew in her heart she had already decided:

I know no one here, but I really want to stay. It seems perfect for what I need right now. I can't believe my guide says I shouldn't stay. Does he honestly care about my future and understand? Does he know how hard it is for me and how few good friends I have? At least, I can make some new friends and build a more impressive, professional profile. I want to be taken seriously and respected for the work I do. I deserve a chance to measure up to others or at least look like I do. Still, I do want to get to my Summit and don't want to be stuck.

She looked once more at that morning's note:

```
Your time is your most valued possession. Stay on
course and don't let any fabricated validation distract
you from your purpose. Just as a bridge needs to be
solidly built, so do segments in your life. Don't let
anything hinder you from getting to your destination.
```

She quickly bolted the door for the night and after closing her journal, she laid down on the cot. Crockett had pulled off one of the blankets to lie on. She dreamed of flying on the trapeze, but after she caught her partner's hands, she didn't remember anything else.

CHAPTER NINE

The Roundabout

Light streamed in the room as she awoke from a fitful night's sleep where in one dream, a trapeze artist fell from the highwire, hurtling toward his death. In another, a menacing clown with a black garish smile chased her in and out of circus tents. Upon waking, relieved, she found Crockett still by her side. Quickly, she threw on her clothes to get ready for the "Need Friends" seminar. For the first time, the table sat bare with no breakfast. Undaunted, she grabbed a protein bar from her bag. It would have to do. Then she dug out some treats for Crockett. Her mother's photo dropped out. She turned it over to read the now familiar words: *I have always believed that you had everything within you to be successful. You now possess the gems that will help you unlock even more of your future.* The gems! Yes, she still had the amethyst and the emerald. She took them out and marveled at their beauty in the reflected sunlight. Then, she re-read the note contained with the amethyst:

> Purple is a color of royalty. Your experience will give you additional status and power as you use your unique skills.

Immediately another note fluttered to the floor, the one, she had kept safely pressed between the pages of her journal:

> You have already used the key that will help you most, "Courage," but don't forget you have everything within you to continue your journey. Write about the courage you feel and your experience every day in your journal.

She would continue her journey to her Summit for sure. But the circus was an opportunity she didn't want to pass up. The thought crossed her mind that if there was a short-term position available at the city office, even for a couple weeks, she may not have to sell one of her jewels. They could use her remodeling skills. She'd make a quick stop there on her way.

According to the note, the purple stone was about status and power since purple, rare and valuable in ancient times, was reserved for kings and emperors. Royalty, she wasn't, but she hoped that by returning to the photo ops tents, connections and friend possibilities would increase her prominence. She couldn't wait until some of her family members saw her new posts. She wanted to explore her possibilities without any more distractions.

Gathering her bag, Mallery made her way to the city office. In its dark interior, several people huddled over their desks surrounded by mounds of paperwork. When she asked if there were any short-term projects for temp work, she only got a head nod. After waiting fifteen minutes for answers, she moved on. She was well-qualified for a short-term position and felt confident they could use her skills. She quickly passed the Seminar Clone Factory and the Styleless Music Shop, where she could hear the same vocal phrases that she had heard the day before. While there, she noticed a vacancy posted for a pet-friendly lodging located close to the circus. She would go there right after the "Need Friends" seminar. Slinging her bag back over her shoulder, she noticed the Band of Hope on her wrist was hanging loosely, almost falling off. She wondered if she had lost weight, which wouldn't be all that bad.

Crockett now pulled her toward the roundabout and jumped into a vehicle in the crowded circular path. "Good boy! You've got the hang of this!" The roundabout seemed larger and busier than yesterday. "Take me to FriendLand!" got no response from her car. They were pushed toward the middle lane by a clown in full costume, hurrying by. She was glad she couldn't see his face as the vision of her nightmarish dream resurfaced.

"Go to FriendLand!" Other workers all stood at the curb, waiting to get on and off. The cars easily responded to their commands. However, though Mallery continued to yell, there was no response to "Go to Bluebird!" or "Go to Tinsel-cam!"

"Crockett, did you give our car a lesson on selective hearing?" Crockett put his paws over his face and sank lower into the vehicle. "I didn't mean to scold you, boy!" She petted him gently. Just then, an attractive woman she recognized as an influencer cut right in front of her and exited. The back of her shirt said, "Need Friends?" Mallery yelled, "Yes!" She commanded her vehicle to get over a lane, and she practically jumped out of her seat when the car swerved, nearly getting sideswiped by a faster vehicle. This time, a dreadful looking clown gave her a wide, sinister smile, just like the clown in her dream. Her startled scream sent Crockett to the floorboards.

As she gave the car instructions, they advanced, swerving between different shaped vehicles. The more she tried to get off, though, the more she was pushed back toward the middle. A large production truck cut in front of her with "Stories for Sale" signs on the sides and back. The driver looked like the woman from the makeup chair the previous day, but more like her original photo, sporting an extra chin without the scarf. "This is an act. It's all an act!" Mallery realized that she was caught in a cycle that would keep her stuck. She remembered the note:

> Don't let any fabricated validation distract you from your purpose.

Her car kept circling. The other passengers had no problem cutting her off or lurching ahead to their exits. Her panic escalated as her vehicle sped faster and faster on the roundabout, like spinning on an out-of-control carousel with clowns, jugglers, acrobats, and magicians, all looking at her with disdain. She had been so sure of her decision the night before, but doubt was creeping into her thoughts, and a dog crouched on the floorboard was no help. Her car kept turning, jostling, and jolting her as they rotated in the middle. The menacing clown glared at her from the roundabout's center pavilion each time she circled. Some strange force wanted her to stay and give up her destination goals. It brought back the unattainable feeling she had about failing to compete with the beautiful people.

Amazingly, the people on the sidelines no longer looked so appealing and alluring. This realization wasn't just because she felt dizzy from the endless circling. Their confident expressions were an illusion, only a cloak of pretense plastered on their faces. Cagney, Treston, and Tamma could have easily been standing right there with them. Why hadn't she seen this truth before? It felt like the clarity and confidence she had gained from her bridge building disappeared, erased like the drawings on an Etch A Sketch. She grabbed a chocolate chip crunch crescent cookie. Now, she was glad she had packed them.

She knew in her heart that she felt fear. During the countless times she faced many of her family members and friends, she avoided the risk of sharing about her dreams and aspirations. The few friends she could count on now seemed even farther away. Once she returned home, she would take the initiative to contact them again. Still the car circled, shoving her sideways but never exiting. Seeing others exit easily escalated a sense of panic.

"I have a defective car!" She had to get off this endless cycle. Lunchtime had come and gone hours ago, and the cookies weren't helping her think clearly. She needed help but then remembered the rest of the note included with the amethyst stone:

Think through all the areas of your experience as you will waste nothing. You will find ways to connect your experience with your skills and what you truly love to do. This combination will create multiple ideas and possibilities for your future.

Experience and skill, what good would those do for her now? Her unique talents couldn't get her off this roundabout. Just yesterday, she had felt every new turn had heightened her sense of adventure with its welcoming invitations and bright lights. Today, she saw only drab outlines of tents and buildings with a grey blanket of dusk settling in. In the land of online connections, the synergy came from a land of mediocrity and superficiality. Why had the car commands worked to get her off the roundabout just a day earlier?

"The commands!" She shouted it so loudly that Crockett lifted his head. "I know what to do." The commands to get off at FriendLand or Tinsel-cam didn't work because she wasn't supposed to go to those places. She was going to her Summit, not to the Social Media Circus. A clear command had to come for the destination that would make a difference in her life. Although she hadn't seen the summit sign, she gave the command.

"Go to the Summit." The car kept circling, so she tried more loudly. "Go to the Summit." The car slowed slightly. With all the confidence and volume, she could produce, she shouted clearly, "I want to go to the Summit!" With this last command, Crockett climbed from the floorboards into the seat. He saw the horror-movie black Cheshire-cat smile of the menacing clown, who leered at them still from the roundabout's center and started barking ferociously. The clown jumped back, then ran across the lanes on foot with cars screeching to barely miss hitting him. Then it appeared, the sign, "To the Summit," just like Mallery had seen the previous day. "That awful clown was hiding the sign, Crockett! Good boy, you gave him a scare!" The sign also said, "Toll required." Even though she had no idea how she'd pay, she needed to exit. With the next revolution, a faded arrow appeared that pointed to a narrow path in the center of the roundabout. In faded print it read, "Roundabout Hero Lane."

"Go to the Summit." She spoke with confidence. It would be a tricky exit since she could see no farther than the sign. "Trust," she said to herself. The car suddenly jerked, turning sharply toward the center of the roundabout. The path came into clearer view as they descended through a dark tunnel on Roundabout Hero Lane. The car then accelerated out of the tunnel, through a cluster of overgrown bushes, revealing a twilight glow in the open sky. The toll booth appeared beyond a group of trees. A tall gate stood at a road that descended further into another tunnel. An electronic kiosk stood between them and the large gate.

A toll meant a fee, but how would she pay? The directions said no cash needed for this journey, and she couldn't imagine using credit. Was she stuck? How could she get around it? For someone good at coding and computers, there had to be a hack to bypass the payment machine to open the gate. This hack had been used at some tollways, according to an article in one of her tech magazines. Up close, the kiosk looked unusual with no opening to put cash or credit cards. Its front contained a rusted metal box with a rectangular hole. A purple glow radiated from the interior.

She shivered, knowing her beautiful amethyst was rectangular. Could she give it up for a silly kiosk? Would it work anyway? The toll machine could gobble up her stone, and she'd be left stranded, trapped in the dark. Why go further if she had to give up everything along the way? Her guide said she had everything to finish her trip, but now she questioned his logic. As an efficient accountant, she had common sense. But many parts of this journey were outside the realm of logic. Her guide had told her in the forest when Treston appeared, "You will become stronger as you overcome each obstacle." He had also asked her, "Have you changed your mind about going to the Summit?" Her reply had always been a resounding, "No."

Was she ready to give up now? She didn't think so. But why had she come? There wasn't time for thinking anymore. The kiosk waited. She looked at the loose Hope band on her wrist and remembered her guides' words, "Persistence will help you build your strengths to make you even stronger. Avoid shells that can be easily broken." Now she was at a dead end. She remembered her mother's words: *You now possess the gems that will help you unlock even more of your future.*

She had given up the sapphire, the ruby, and now was asked to give up the amethyst. Surrendering the gem seemed the only way to enter this gate. Shivering from the cold and indecision, with darkness approaching, she needed some resolve. Persistence. That's what it was going to take. Despite having now eaten a full large bag of chocolate chip crunch crescent cookies, she still felt hungry. However, she was not giving up. Digging in her backpack, she pulled out the precious amethyst, her birthstone, and felt its smooth surface and precise facets. Its configuration matched the box opening. She tentatively inserted the jewel into the rectangular slot where it dropped with a thunk on the metal. Within moments, the gate opened.

"Aaah." Relief and joy replaced the fear and dread she had been holding inside. The gate opening was confirmation that she was on the right path. The band tightened on her wrist. Her small car jolted forward as the gate quickly closed. As they descended underground, a few lights lit the tunnel, leaving them in the semi-darkness. Crockett sat up as the starry night shone through the tunnel exit. He had slept through the whole kiosk ordeal. The little car took them from the tunnel, around a curve, and up to a lone building. "Civilization!" How far had they traveled from the Social Media Circus, Mallery wondered?

Without waiting for her, Crockett jumped from the car and stood by the front door of the looming building. Gathering her backpack, she followed her dog while the car sped into the night. She pulled up to peer into a window. There was no one in sight. Crockett gave her an encouraging lick as she knocked on the door. No one answered, but the door opened easily with one turn of its knob. Crockett bounded in with a single leap. She tentatively followed, beholding a meal on the table with delicious aromas and sighed in relief. In her journal, she wrote her thoughts:

> I can't believe I'm here, safe and warm for the night after such an awful day. I thought I had made the right decision but realize now how little I control my circumstances. I was afraid of missing out. But I was so wrong in not trusting the advice from my guide. A lane called "Roundabout Hero" led me from endless circling onto a clear path toward my destination. But only after I focused on the greater purpose of my journey, which was to find out who I could really become by making it to my Summit. That was the reason why I came, and it hasn't changed. But there must be more.

Crockett had found his bowl of food and had curled up on a dog bed in the corner. She wanted to do the same, but had to write more:

> Even though today did not go well, I can start again tomorrow. I want to chase after what is real and find it in my Summit.

It felt good to curl up beneath the thick heavy blankets. She fell into a deep sleep without a single thought of evil clowns, threatening vehicles, or bright flashing lights.

CHAPTER TEN

The Dangers of Distraction

Mallery awakened as sunlight streamed through the front window. The breakfast waiting on the table looked inviting, but before eating, she recorded her still-fresh thoughts about the previous day:

Yesterday turned out differently than I had expected. I thought it was a good idea to spend time at a place where I could boost my profile, add friends, and expand my influence. It doesn't seem fair that I ended up stuck, circling endlessly on a roundabout and saw no one else in the same predicament. Others got on and off easily while nothing worked for me except directing my commands to go to the Summit while I focused on the greater purpose of my journey.

This last phrase reminded her how much easier it seemed for others to get the huge break, big promotion, or new relationship that increased their status. That had never happened for her:

Will I ever get a chance again to build connections and expand my influence like in the Social Media Circus? I can't imagine finding that place again. But part of me realizes it may not be real. My thoughts and imagination have turned into a jumble of crossed wires and detours as there are parts of this journey that cannot be logically explained. Although I did eat a whole bag of cookies, which made me feel dumpy. That was real.

She smiled because she wanted to re-read her words when she found herself confused, depressed, or bored. It would straighten her thoughts when tempted to repeat her bad habits. The message in the front of her journal was a good reminder:

`Thoughts become clearer when you state them and then communicate them.`

She wolfed down her tasty, familiar breakfast of granola, fruit, and roll, thankful for its predictability. As she pondered her experience at the Social Media Circus, she recalled the empty, dust-filled tables in the Idea Factory. She reviewed the pictures of her bridge handiwork. If it wasn't destroyed, it would be there for others to cross:

As I look at pictures of my work, I'm surprised at what I accomplished. Just as there was abandoned work left undone in the Idea Factory, I have also abandoned some ideas still hidden away. Maybe I'll share them when I return and encourage others to do the same. I have been focusing on where I want to be, fighting the feeling that I couldn't measure up with all the professional accomplishments and perfect profiles of people around me. But

I want to focus on what's ahead and how I am different. I have unique skills and abilities, and I have learned important principles in using them. If I consistently build on my unique skills, I will stand out as someone different and innovative.

As she read her words aloud to herself, she added,

I love designing and building. I wonder if this will be something I can do when I return. I will make a goal of designing something small or using an engineering principle every day so I will be better equipped. And maybe, just maybe, I won't feel as unfortunate as the meaning of my name, Mallery.

Before putting her journal away, she sketched a safer exit off the round-about. With her plan, the sharp turn they had taken would no longer be needed. It would still be discreet with the surrounding bushes and trees, though she'd create a larger "Roundabout Hero" sign to make it clearer. She would show her design to her guide, certain it would work.

"So what's next?" Crockett, his head in her lap, waited for a treat. Would her guide show up and fill her in? Crockett ate a piece of her breakfast roll. Mallery stepped outside the cabin and whiffed the fresh air. It felt good even though a dead-end road lay beyond the door.

"It would be nice to stay here another day, but I won't." Crockett whined. He wanted a head rub. A sign at the end of the road said, "Hero Mountain Summit Straight Ahead." All she could see was a narrow dirt path. "I guess we'd better get going, Crockett. Not much of a trail, but if the sign says that's the way, we have to believe it will lead us to the Summit." He followed as she went back inside to gather her belongings. She stopped to write one more line in her journal:

Today, I will again be walking forward, trusting the sign before me to lead to my Summit. Trust is not easy for me. We'll see where this narrow path takes us today. Hopefully I won't repeat yesterday's "Day of Distraction."

With that, she put her journal in her backpack, grabbed the lunch sack, and, looking once more around the cozy room, walked down the front steps. The trail looked clear beyond the Hero Mountain Summit sign. "Day of Distraction" was a better depiction over of a "Day of Lost Opportunity." The trees, tall and swaying in the breeze, provided a boundary of protection. The well-kept path ahead was not revealed on her map. The maintenance of the trail reminded her how much work her mother put in managing her small garden at home. Did her mother know about her journey? With the beauty around her, Mallery felt compelled to sing. Although she didn't like her voice, it felt right to burst into song with Crockett as her audience:

I am on a journey; this is my Summit song. When will I be there? I hope it won't be long.

When her guide suddenly appeared, she stopped her song, embarrassed. Did he hear her singing?

"This is the last leg of your trip. If you stay on course, you'll get to the Summit." His words gave her hope. Even though she'd messed up, he hadn't abandoned her. Now, she was back on track. The Band of Hope felt snug on her wrist. She resisted giving him a big hug and quickened her steps, though she wanted to run. Calmly he said, "There will be more challenges. Here are your tools," as he handed over a medium-sized bag.

"Whoa! What are these?" She sat on a rock to look inside.

"A rope, carabiners, hammer, and pitons." He saw her furrowed brow, "Pitons are climbing pegs."

Mallery couldn't quit staring at the contents. He continued, "You do have to *climb* a mountain."

"These are *serious* climbing tools. I've never done mountain climbing before. People die on mountains, you know."

"You could have died on the bridge, too, but you didn't. Trust the process."

There it was again, "Trust." She had recommitted just this morning to scale her Summit – no turning back. "What are these ribbons for?"

"You had some wilderness training, right?"

"Right. They're trail markers. I remember that from my childhood scout group."

"They will not only to help you find your way but also ensure that you won't lose your way." In scouts, tying ribbons around trees in their campsites had felt like a game. She could easily follow them back after a hike. But this was different.

"So, I should place markers on the path ahead?"

Her guide was smiling, "They will come in handy."

Mallery pictured herself getting lost, then imagined herself dangling from a rope off the mountainside.

"Even if you don't like heights, just keep moving and don't let your imagination run away with you."

"A run-away Imagination is the least of my worries." Mallery went on, "This is real danger, especially if I have to hang from a rope off a vertical edge." Her heart beat faster just thinking of it.

"I know you're afraid, Mallery." The bag of tools felt heavier in her lap. The guide continued, "You still want to get to the Summit, correct?"

"Correct, definitely correct!" Her answer came more quickly than her confidence.

"Then I will see you at the top," he said, then disappeared in the trees.

She stood still, gathering her thoughts. Crockett had remained at her feet the whole time, calm as ever.

"Crockett, old boy, what was I thinking?" Looking at her traveling companion reminded her that *they* had gotten this far. Crockett was not going to quit, for every day held new adventures for him. But if she had to climb the face of a mountain, how would Crockett make the climb? "Trust," she said tentatively. After all, she was on the last part of her trip. That, at least, was encouraging. She had already come so far. She took out her journal:

The first part of my trip was through the forest. My purpose became much clearer as I had to choose the better of two paths that would get me to my destination. Treston ran out to stop me, and I got a call from Cagney. It was hard to face them, but it will be much easier now with what I have learned. Then, I had to open doors in what looked like little bunkers, hoping nothing would jump out at me, or worse, that I would get trapped inside of one. With the keys I found, gates opened for me so Crockett and I could walk through a garden as well as a thistle patch. I found my voice with the last gate of courage, especially as I heard my words echoing. I felt confidence that I've not sensed in a long time. Next came the jewels.

She paused, as she thought about the beauty and the sense of loss at having to give them up:

It was dark, cold, and challenging in the cave, but the beautiful stones I uncovered were truly spectacular. They each carried a special message written just for me. Through reading the notes, I realized I have more strengths than I give myself credit for.

The emerald remained in her possession. She hoped that didn't change:

I found a note from my mother. I had no idea she believed in me, and how did she know about the jewels? Could she have taken this same journey at some point? I'm still amazed I was able to build a bridge. But now I remember I had a teacher tell me how I had the ability to look at the physics of a problem from multiple angles. I didn't fully understand the extent of what he said at the time, but I do now. I crossed a bridge that I built!

That thought sent a sense of pride and thankfulness through her. She would call it the "Bridge of Skills."

I don't quite know what else to write about the Social Media Circus except that it felt like a good dream that turned into a nightmare. Even with all the people, I still felt alone and isolated. Part of me wants to fit in and be popular and be pretty. Actually, it's more than that. I want to be respected.

She said the word aloud, "Respected," as Crockett looked up. "You respect me, boy. I know you do." He jumped up and licked her on her cheek, barely missing her mouth. She laughed, knowing she was different. She resolved not to abandon her ideas like those forgotten in the dusty Idea Factory.

Writing in her journal reset her focus. She wondered how many more obstacles she would face and secretly hoped to find the pinnacle without having to scale the face of a mountain. If she could look at the physics of a problem from multiple angles, maybe she could find another way of climbing. Did reaching the top really require rappelling on ropes? She would take time to think as she moved forward. The Band of Hope felt warm and firm. It had become a source of comfort, though in a way she couldn't express. Did it hold some uncanny power? With all the strange happenings like finding places to stay, along with meals and jewels, it was entirely possible.

As Mallery reread her journal, she recalled how far she had come both in distance and in self-awareness. She decided not to count the number of days she had been gone. As time had slowed, she didn't want to speed it up, at least not until she figured out a path to her Summit. Putting her journal and tools in her backpack, she set off, determined, but dreading the mountain ahead. Her thoughts became consumed with multiple plans for some gondolas to scale a mountain.

CHAPTER ELEVEN

The Wings of Hope

The path curved sharply to her left. The large, flat cobblestones looked hand-hewn, chiseled to interlock, creating an artistic mosaic. Most were partially covered with a thick layer of dirt, but she could still see their pattern. As Mallery and Crockett progressed, the path became clearer with more stones peeking through the dirt and moss until they reached an open space. Crockett jumped up and swallowed a bug, but Mallery held him back, not wanting to take a break or a detour. The road ahead curved to the right, in another arc. Flocks of birds chattered as they flew across the meadow, and the yellow wildflowers, Bermuda buttercup, stood in full bloom. Why would a path be crafted with such artful stones with only a meadow as its destination? She dreamed of standing at a podium in front of a few hundred people in this meadow. Somehow, that no longer seemed completely impossible, especially if she was surrounded by beauty like this.

Once again along the trail, the trees became thick, nearly blocking the light on the stone path. Above a thick mass of branches, a village appeared on the horizon, which explained this road of cobblestones. But it had quickly disappeared, making her think it was a mirage. She rounded another curve in what seemed a familiar pattern. Was she circling? Would the hideous clown's smile soon flash before her? If she had to leave this dead-end path, where would she go?

She had heard of haunted forests, so her imagination went into overdrive, especially as she remembered the terror of the roundabout. It was silly to let her analytical mind wander there, but it wasn't just a frightened feeling. It was a sense of isolation and desertion, being separated from friends, even her acquaintances. She wished to dismiss these thoughts but couldn't muster the will to do so. An owl hooted overhead, as a bird swooped to tease Crockett. Her body jerked to attention. Narrow footpaths ahead offered no directional signs to guide her, and these paths disappeared into another thick grove of trees.

No backtracking, she decided. If the path ahead was clear, she would stay on it. As the afternoon wore on, she kept her eyes open for a mountain. Two energetic squirrels provided no sense of where she was or what to do next, but they kept Crockett busy. They flicked their tails, squeaking in squirrel-chatter, teasing him by running up and down trees they knew he couldn't access. She distracted herself by identifying the pine trees with their needle-like clusters and cones. She was thankful for her wilderness training. The variety of stones were beautiful, too, but Mallery still felt lost. Evening was imminent. Where was she?

She stood on a large rock and looked far beyond the trees. The scene seemed oddly familiar. She had indeed been circling! This time, she would go toward the village and hope it wasn't a mirage. Even though no clear road signs appeared, she continued. The squirrels re-appeared, mocking Crockett. She felt like letting him off his leash in revenge, but they ran away through a cluster of ferns. Crockett pulled her with him, sure that he'd catch the dynamic duo, taking her with him through the fronds. "This looks like Cinnamon Fern, Crockett." He wasn't interested at all. He wanted those squirrels. Crockett deserved a treat for following the squirrels to find the type of fern that intrigued her, and he happily chomped on his prize as Mallery distracted him with a treat.

Mallery had kept the fern she found in the cave for her mother, so finding the same fern here was curious. Was this a sign? As she stooped among the ferns, she saw a path, entirely overgrown by dense underbrush, like a mountain bike trail. She took a stem of the fern to match the other piece she had kept when finding the emerald. As she dug in her bag, her hand fell first on the bag of ribbons. "Ribbons! That's it." She could mark the path with colorful ties, making it easier to find her way back if she got lost to indicate if she was truly circling. The original fern frond was still as green as when she first picked it. The realization that the fern had inexplicably kept its color and that she had ribbons encouraged Mallery. She firmly tied a red ribbon on a branch, as she stepped over knotted roots and red manzanita branches. "C'mon Crockett, this way." At the next curve, she tied a blue ribbon around a bush and additional ribbons as she continued. The path soon became more open and looked well-traveled.

Then, after a few more yards, the travelers came upon an obstruction, a felled tree and bits of underbrush across the walkway. At the same time, the sky was darkening with the onset of dusk. Should she keep going or head back to the main road, she wondered. Crockett pulled her ahead, just like he had done in the cave. She felt the firm grip of the Band of Hope on her wrist, an assurance she needed more than ever. She wanted to prove that Craven, Cagney, Treston, and Shamere were wrong about her. They'd always be a part of her world, but she didn't need to recall their negative, disparaging remarks at this moment.

It was strange, the colorful ribbons felt like new little friends to help her find her way. That made no logical sense in her analytical mind, but it felt good. Just then, a glimmer of light shone through the dense forest. She pushed ahead through the intertwined roots. Crockett didn't mind the challenge or the darkness as his nose was leading the way. He pulled hard against her, jumping forward. As the dog jerked the leash out of her hand, she fell forward into a ravine. Although she tried to shield her fall by rolling, she landed on her arm that was still tender from her fall on the bridge. She didn't move, mostly from the shock and felt unsure about getting up.

"The last thing I need now is to twist an ankle or break an arm." A feeling of impending doom threatened her, but Crockett came to her side, trying to make up with a slobbery lick. She couldn't be mad at her traveling companion, for he wouldn't leave her. She wiggled her toes, moved her legs, and realized nothing was broken. Slowly getting on her knees, she grasped Crockett's collar, and the dog pulled her out. As they resumed their walk, a light appeared, showing a cabin in the distance. Moss covered the sides of the structure, its shingles clinging loosely to the roof with others scattered on the ground. With relief and gratitude, Mallery let Crockett lead the way to the rustic front door, half covered with a thick vine. She pulled vegetation away as she turned the knob. The door opened easily. The light inside the minimally furnished room revealed a table and a cot in the corner, a sight both reassuring and familiar. The table held a container that she guessed held her dinner. She'd be fed and sheltered for another night. How did her guide get here before her?

A ladder in the back of the room led to a second level, perhaps a loft or attic, but it was not well-lit. She would wait until morning to climb and explore because her knee hurt. Crockett ate the dogfood he found in the corner then rested his head in her lap.

"You're not getting any of my food tonight, Crockett. You've had enough." As if he could understand, he gave her a good nuzzle and went to pout on the dog-bed. She took out her journal to write her thoughts:

I am so happy to be okay after what could have happened. My body hurts, but I have no broken bones, and my arm is just extra-sore from a hard fall. Once again, I am in a place I did not expect to find, containing food and shelter for the night. The fact that my guide gave me ribbons made me feel secure, confident, and not alone in my journey. Maybe it's because I'm finally at the last part of my trip and am feeling hope for the future instead of regret for the past. I want to remember this feeling because others may be in the same place, feeling alone without the promise of something better. I, at least, want to give them a glimpse of what can be though I'm not at the top yet. I am still thinking of another way to get to my Summit besides climbing a mountain with carabiners and ropes. There is a ladder here, and I hope it's sturdy enough to give me a better view of the area from a second story elevation. If what I saw was a village, I want to see more of it.

She reflected for a moment. But there was more she needed to say:

I have recently questioned why I wanted to come on this trip in the first place. Most of all, I wanted to prove that I could do it on my own, not only to myself but also to my family and friends. I have accomplished that much by getting this far. Now I'm feeling something more significant but can't explain it yet. But I no longer want to be called Mallery, the disadvantaged. I don't want to be like everyone else. From what I saw at the Social Media Circus, there was plenty of copycat thinking. I want to think for myself and show the world the real me. Until now, I've only wanted to fit in. If I can make it to my Summit, I know I am good enough. I won't listen to the other voices that say I'm not. I can make it all the way.

With that burst of confidence, she put away her journal, ate the fresh meal provided, and lay on the cot. A deep sleep soon took over her thoughts.

Morning came with filtered sunlight streaming in the window, and she woke refreshed. The ladder in the corner made her eager to explore where it went. The bowl of grains, fruit, and a breakfast roll on the table would have to wait. The ladder rungs, old and splintered, held her. The extensions at the top looked high, quite a bit beyond the level visible from the floor. Her knees felt strong enough to carefully step on each rung. After ascending ten steps, she held onto the crossbeam. Would this be like climbing to her Summit? If so, she could handle it. One rung at a time. Just then, a rung gave way. Her hands slipped, giving her palm a good-sized splinter. "Darn!"

She heard Crockett whimper below. "I'm okay, just a little stumble." She didn't dare look down.

Crockett was now lying at the foot of the ladder. "You don't like heights either, do you boy?" Another ten rungs brought her to an additional platform with a window at its edge. Checking each rung thoroughly, feeling the equal pressure on both feet for balance, she gingerly put her weight on the platform. Nothing moved, making her thankful for her deft ability to logically assess weight. She had taken this ability for granted, but it had become apparent on this trip, particularly in bridge-building. When her boss had affirmed her exact computations on the extra side projects, she hadn't thought much of it. Now, she was grateful. Looking out of the window from this third-level viewpoint, she saw another dense clump of trees on one side of the cabin. On the other far side, a beautifully crafted cobblestone lane led to a village in the distance.

"There is a village!" A few ant-like objects she knew had to be people were moving out and about in its streets. Even from this distance, they moved purposefully. "Out for morning walks, no doubt." She couldn't wait to join them. Then she gasped, for beyond the village rose the outline of a mountain! The remote peak stood magnificently, radiating soft shades of pink, yellow, and purple. Its aura kept her eyes transfixed, so majestic, inspiring, grand, and uplifting. To reach the top would be an unforgettable experience. How strange that she could only see the mountain from her elevated vantage point. However, she closed her eyes and imagined herself at the top, victorious in her climb. Then reality hit. What was she thinking? The mountain looked ominous. She slowly descended the ladder, careful of the loose rung, and Crockett greeted her with licks when she reached the floor. After removing the splinter, she sat down to breakfast.

"Okay boy. You were patient." She threw her dog a morsel of her breakfast roll. She wanted to get going, but felt the need to write first:

I just had a glimpse of the mountain peak, my Summit. I am overwhelmed with not only the beauty of the mountain, but also that it's within my grasp. I was hoping the climb would be more like stepping up the rungs of a ladder, but it will take more to get to the top. I could not have gotten this far without my guide. I hope I have everything necessary to get to the top. The fact that I've had to carry these climbing tools tells me there probably won't be any sort of lift or shortcuts. I must do the work. Climbing to the top will be the hardest thing I've ever done.

Mallery grabbed her bag but there was one more line:

... I have confidence.

That last statement took trust with a sprinkle of faith, but she wanted to think positively. Mallery packed her bag and grabbed Crockett's leash. "Time to go." She set out on the cobblestone road ahead. The thick foliage on the far side of the cabin hindered her way. She once again tied ribbons on trees to mark the route. She pretended she was placing stakes and ribbons to visualize the layout for a new building project. These were her new friends. From her viewpoint from the ladder, the road had looked much closer. When she saw no sign of it, she hoped it hadn't been a figment of her imagination.

A flicker of light sparked through the trees, then disappeared. It looked nothing like a town ahead. It blinked again like it could be a firefly, but they didn't show up this early in the day. Once Crockett had seen it, he pulled her toward the shiny glint that grew brighter as she approached. She pulled back on the leash with yesterdays' fall fresh in her memory.

"Slow, boy. Let's see what this is." She took a few steps and focused on a very small object hanging from a branch, a sparkling clump of glitter. "Wow! How beautiful!" A crystalline sac with a single wing was attached to a tree branch, the cocoon of an emerging butterfly struggling to free itself. Mallery had studied the process of metamorphosis in school, but this cocoon seemed different. A light shone from the inside of the sac, like the interior of a small home. All the lights inside would be extinguished when the butterfly fully emerged to spread its wings and fly. As she watched the movement, Mallery struggled along with the butterfly but dared not touch it. It needed to push the fluid out of its body into its wings to survive. If she tried to help, it wouldn't live.

"Hold still, Crockett." They both stood frozen as spectators. Watching the high-wire act at the Social Media Circus with trapeze artists flying effortlessly was nothing like the struggle before her. In the same way, her journey had not been easy. But she, too, needed to fly, just like that butterfly. She didn't need to measure up to anyone else's definition of success. Just then, the butterfly emerged, flitted around her with a radiant glow and flew upward, absorbing the cocoon's glow in its wings as it fluttered among the highest tree branches. Mallery, having shed her cocoon, wanted to fly just as high. The shiny winged creature headed toward the path.

"Crockett, let's follow," pulling his leash toward the butterfly's direction. A few flat stones, buried in the dirt, became a wider, clearer pathway. The butterfly led them forward, with glistening wings flitting up and down on the trail, while Mallery held tight to Crockett's leash. The cobblestone pavers were not a figment of her imagination. Their intricate craftsmanship reflected the artistry involved in creating a beautiful passage that felt magical. The butterfly and the pavers held the promise of the village ahead. She started singing a revised version of her song to fit her mood:

I am on a journey; this is my Summit song.
I will soon be there; I know it won't be long.

She sang it over until she came to a roundabout with a sign that said, "Town Center." She saw people on the surrounding streets. She hoped to ask someone about getting to the mountain as soon as possible. Mallery took in the view.

"What a beautiful place." Though she could not locate this town on her map, it had to be real. Many people were riding bikes. With a bike, she could reach the mountain's base more quickly, but then there was the climb. What would she do with Crockett?

"Let's go." The village shopfronts looked old and full of romance, like ones in travel brochures. One shop, tall and narrow, had large windows with a sign that read, "Summit Climbing Gear." Ropes hung beside dangling objects in the front display, but the door notice said it wouldn't open for another thirty minutes. This would be a place to get the information for her climb. The street held other small shops. Bella's Brooches Baubles and Beads displayed brooches, earrings, bracelets, and rings on velvet cards. Workers at Crispy Crumble Confections were putting out fresh cupcakes. Mallery's stomach growled. She could hardly pull Crockett away from their sweet aroma. There must be a lake with all the people waiting for Trout's Tackle and Bait to open its doors.

Mallery wondered how many from the Idea Factory had left their towns to come here. The Fantasy and Fables Used Books would attract artists and creative types. She would love to peruse the shelves. Then, rows of bikes stood in front of the Pedal Pusher Cycle Shop. She circled back to the Summit Climbing Gear shop, now open. A sign said, "Training and Teams" and pictured different weights of ropes, multi-colored carabiners, belts, and clothing. A bell on the door rang as she entered. The man behind the counter had a familiar look with kind eyes, like her guide. His presence reassured her though she didn't know why.

"Who's this big buddy?"

"His name is Crockett." The man grabbed a dog treat from behind the counter, "Here Crockett. Good boy," he crooned, as he stroked the dog's head.

"I want to get to my Summit. Is that it in the distance?"

"Yes, that's Hero Mountain, known as The Summit."

"Where can I get information? I have no experience in mountain climbing. What's involved?"

"Why do you want to reach your Summit?"

This question caught her off guard. Why would a simple shop owner need to know? Shouldn't he be selling her equipment? He seemed to read her thoughts.

"Not everyone makes it. Many start their climb but never finish."

"Why? Did they die?"

"Oh no, they just quit. It's safe if you know what you're doing and have the right team."

"What do you mean by 'the right team'?"

"You can't get there on your own. You need a reliable, trustworthy team to help you."

"I don't know anyone here, that is, besides my guide. But he's not around much." She could see the twinkle in the shopkeeper's eye. "I have friends who say they made it, but I don't believe them. Maybe they really quit."

"Your instincts are probably right."

"I want not only to prove that I can do it but also to find who I can become."

"The climb is difficult. Even though you may have the right gear, you have to prepare mentally for the climb."

"With confidence, right?"

"Yes, confidence helps. But there will be times when you will slip, times when you'll be exhausted, and times when you will fear. You'll think you can't go any further, but that's the time to push forward. Since there is a safety rope to take you down, many choose the easier path to the bottom and think they'll try it again. But they never do."

Mallery sighed more loudly than she expected at this bad news. She tried to focus her thoughts but could feel her resolve slipping away with the same doubt, fear, and uncertainty that had plagued her the entire trip. After all, her name was Mallery, the disadvantaged, unfortunate one.

"So why do you want to make this climb?" Why was he pressing her? Could she verbalize her growing sense of confidence and firm intention to succeed? This man seemed kind. She remembered the words she wrote the previous night:

I must do the work. Climbing to the top will be the hardest thing I've ever done.

Then she remembered the beautiful butterfly, its struggle and the freedom to fly. Looking into the man's face, she had no answer. Hearing the strenuous description from this shop owner, who was familiar with the climb, felt different from hearing one of her friends warn her.

"I ... I know it won't be easy." Then, the words came to her that she had written so confidently in her journal:

The fact that I've had everything I've needed so far for my trip gives me confidence that I will find what I need when I get to the base of the mountain.

She knew that response didn't answer his question, so she made another attempt, "I need to try for me, to prove to myself I have the strength to make my Summit and fly. What else do I need to prepare?"

His smile made her relax, as if he knew exactly what she would ask. He brought a booklet out from behind the counter like the one her guide had given her about building a bridge though this cover was dark green instead of blue.

"This booklet will tell what you need to know. Most people think they can make it on their own and don't ask for help. You've taken an important first step."

"Thank you so much." She grabbed Crockett's leash and stepped outside. Making her way down the street, she looked inside the booklet. At a small outdoor table at the Sumptuous and Savory Sidewalk Café, she grabbed a seat and ordered a latté. The outline of the distant mountain looked threatening from this viewpoint. It felt much easier to write in her journal this morning than realize that she soon would be taking the next step, starting the climb.

As she opened the book, the chapter titles jumped out at her: **"Weight and Balance," "Best Equipment,"** and **"Reasons for Failure."** She took out the bright blue book she had kept on building a bridge. The chapters were almost the same. Maybe the underlying principles were similar? She looked back at her journal entries:

The intricate balance of a bridge is possible because of equally weighted sections that hold up under pressure. Part of the intricate balance of life is adding in sections of equal weight that will hold up under pressure.

There was that word, "pressure." Was she letting pressure influence her? She had dismissed outside pressure from family and friends to succeed, but maybe she was putting more pressure on herself than she realized. She had also written:

If I can identify what parts of my life are carrying extra weight, I can balance them more easily not to feel like I'll crash with exhaustion, stress, or discouragement.

She couldn't let the weight of stress and pressure hold her down, especially when climbing a mountain. The shopkeeper had said, "You have to prepare mentally for the climb." How much mental preparation did she need? She would have to keep her focus on her goal. The emerald's message was "never quit. Never, never quit." Since she still had the emerald, maybe it would empower her. The next chapter on best equipment was like the best materials in building her bridge. She had the climbing gear her guide had given her, but she wondered what else she would need. The bridge book had said, "Choose materials after anticipating the force of the load." At the shop, she saw materials available for climbing, including different sizes of ropes, carabiners, hooks, and even survival equipment. She would have to depend on the expert advice of the shopkeeper to get everything she needed. After the equipment came a section that went a step further. The booklet described how teams climbed together and that a minimum of a week was involved for the training.

This provoked more questions. Who would she climb with and where would she stay? She didn't know anyone in this little town and had just met the shopkeeper. As she slowly sipped her latté, she read about successful climbers. There was a jewelry maker from the Far East, a builder from a town just north of her home, a Spanish doctor, all from different walks of life. Why did they make their journey, she wondered? Did they have something to prove like she did? Apparently, they were good enough to reach the top. She wanted to spread her wings, just like that beautiful butterfly, but could she? Would her words ring true?

...the fact that I've had everything I've needed so far for my trip gives me confidence that I will find what I need when I get to the base of the mountain.

To reach her Summit would be the pinnacle of her trip. This section ended with the phrase, "Payment in full is due at the beginning of training." She read that again. She had no idea there would be payment. Wasn't everything covered? She had assumed all fees would be taken care of as part of the journey. She felt like once again she was at the toll booth, needing to pass. She would talk to the shopkeeper about terms after browsing through a few of the local shops.

Crispy Crumble Confections had a "Chocolate Chow Down" doggy treat on the menu. Mallery had to get one for Crockett, which he devoured in two bites. She popped her head into Bella's Brooches Baubles and Beads but decided to come back later. She couldn't concentrate on anything until she talked with the shopkeeper. She was met with a smile at the Summit Climbing Gear Shop and was offered a chair in the corner.

The shopkeeper started, "You probably have questions? Did everything in the booklet make sense?"

"Oh yes. I understand a lot of the basic principles but have no climbing experience. However, it said there's a minimum of a week of training?"

"Yes. We make sure you are ready to be successful." He sounded just like her guide, a resemblance she couldn't help but notice. She tried not to stare and looked away.

"Our next training begins tomorrow."

"Tomorrow? What is the cost? Are there terms available?"

"There are no payment plans." He grabbed a rusted metal box from under the counter. Mallery gasped, her heart in her throat. It looked like the other metal boxes she had seen. On the top was a pear-shaped cutout with an inner green glow. Would her precious emerald be required for this last part of her journey? The stone in the silver pouch was in the familiar pear shape. She stared at the box. She had hoped to keep that gem.

The shopkeeper continued, "This is the only payment accepted."

"I'll be back later."

"Definitely think about it because training's tomorrow. Let me know before the end of the day."

Grabbing Crockett, she kept her composure by leaving the shop. "It's not fair, Crockett." She was glad he led her along, as she felt like folding her wings back into her cocoon. Why did she have to give her last jewel? She had spent all she had to get this far in her journey. She realized the longer she had held on to the gem, the more she had set her heart on keeping the emerald.

CHAPTER TWELVE

The Preparation for The Climb

Tears blurred her vision as she walked up the street. Mallery had faced hardship during this trip and had endured. Now she must make the mountain top, or she would be left with nothing, or would she? Keeping the emerald would prove she had been on an exciting journey. Would getting to the top only give her bragging rights? Would that accomplishment change her life, to bring better friends, find inspiring work, or discover true love? She would, at least, go to the base of Hero Mountain to have a look. Maybe standing there would renew her determination to reach the Summit. She didn't want to become a statistic, one who started the climb, only to give up by sliding down the safety rope. Such cowardice would let her team down. She needed time to think.

"No, not now." Mallery realized the Band of Hope was missing. Did she leave it at the shop or lose it while walking around the village? Crockett's big brown eyes looked attentive, but he probably wanted another doggy treat. "We'll be okay, Crockett, what difference did that wrist band make anyway? Right, boy?" Then, she remembered her guide's warning that she couldn't get to the Summit without hope. Her mind felt cloudy. As she passed the Sumptuous and Savory Café, she saw a couple sitting at the table she had previously occupied.

As a barista approached, she asked, "Did anyone find a small yellow wristband? I was just here a little while ago, and I've lost it."

"Oh, I remember you." He paused, looking at her intently, "Actually, I did find it, but I think I threw it in the trash with some napkins. I'm sorry." Then, he turned, disappearing into the back room while the couple remained at the table. Should she wait for the server to return? She stood paralyzed in the café with her jumbled thoughts. If she didn't make the climb, she'd need a place to stay. However, if she made the climb, what could she do with Crockett? Her thoughts kept spinning with no logical conclusion until the barista returned with a huge smile and a small yellow band.

"Oh, you found my Band of Hope!"

"Your what?"

"It's a special wristband." Slipping it over her hand, she said, "Thank you so much for your trouble."

"It's the least I could do. I threw it away, after all." Their eyes met, and she smiled. He smiled back. He was cute. Maybe she should stay in this town a little longer.

As she left the café, with her mood lifted and mind cleared, she decided to look closer at the mountain face. She followed a side street and ducked behind some tall buildings with deeply sloped roofs. The towering facade of Hero Mountain loomed in the distance. With Crockett by her side, she gazed at a peak rising higher than she had imagined. From her vantage point, she could tell that the rocky face was steep with small crevices and anchor points at various places in the rock.

Her stomach turned at the thought of hanging off one of the ledges, but she didn't feel as frightened as before. She saw movement at the top, which could very well be a group of climbers. She took out her journal:

Hero Mountain is beautiful. None of my friends or Cagney would ever attempt to climb their summit. I want the types of friends who would attempt the climb. For Beeshman, he needs to change his name from "strong" to "coward." But I haven't been much better. My negative self-talk is annoying, just like Cagney could be encouraging in a discouraging way. I don't want to quit. I got this far. I must keep going.

She took the pear-shaped emerald out of her bag. Light bounced off the stone's precise cuts with an intense green radiance. She had never owned anything so magnificent, but her mind was made up. Even if it cost her everything, Mallery wanted to finish her journey. The emerald hadn't been hers to begin with, but now it was hers to invest. She felt the warmth of the Band of Hope, firm on her arm. It was afternoon, so she turned back to the climbing gear shop to see the shopkeeper. For she would start training the next day.

He was smiling when she entered, and she confidently returned his smile.

"So what did you decide?" She took out her precious emerald and with determination, placed it on the counter.

"You won't regret this difficult decision, and you will make it to the top." Hearing those words made her smile easily.

"I hope so." She looked at the magnificent gem. "I felt like I lost part of myself, so I wanted to keep this beautiful stone."

"You will not regret this choice because you'll be equipped to do more than just hang on to a stone that may or may not have great worth." He took out the tin box. Mallery dropped the stone into the pear-shaped opening where it disappeared with a thunk. The shopkeeper then took out a key from under the counter.

"Meet here tomorrow morning. This key is to a cottage in the back. Everything you need is there, and you'll spend the entire week training until the climb begins. We'll provide a dog sitter for Crockett throughout the training and your climb. There's a dog park nearby and plenty of help. He'll be very happy."

"Thank you so much." The tears she felt now were joyful. With a bounce in her step, she walked up the street, relieved she had finalized her choice, knowing all would be taken care of, including Crockett. With the leash looped around her hand, she stretched both arms straight up, looking at the sky. She had never seen answers written there, but the vastness of the blue horizon spoke to her soul of boundless opportunity. The hills surrounding the town were turning bright orange, and their shadows were gradually lengthening.

The Willow and Birch Crafted Carvings shop stood at the end of the street, and Mallery noticed a huge stack of freshly chopped wood under a shed, connected on one side. Under the multi-faceted shingled roof hung a "Pet Friendly" sign, so she and her dog walked in through the ornately carved door. The fresh scent of wood shavings reminded her of the walks she had experienced on her journey, deep in the woods. There were intricately crafted bowls, ornate frames, and hand-hewn statues.

Behind the counter was a large beard, revealing a kind-faced man hardly taller than she. He looked up,

"May I help you?"

"I'm not looking for anything, but your work is extraordinary! These items are beautiful!"

"Thank you. Are you visiting?"

"Yes."

"What a good-looking dog!" He threw Crockett a treat, which the dog gobbled in one gulp. "Will you be climbing the Summit?"

"I will. I'm nervous about the challenge, though." How crazy, she just spoke of this goal to a stranger.

With a knowing smile, he said, "I climbed the Summit some years ago, and it changed my life."

The confused look on her face spurred him to continue.

"I was afraid to pursue my dream of being a woodcarver. Even while growing up, I dreamt of having my own shop. It started with elementary school on a camping trip. I became fascinated by the different wood textures and colors on our hikes. My grandfather had given me a whittling knife, and I made my first bird from a dead branch. It was pretty crude, but then I knew what I wanted to do." He continued, "After finishing school, I worked for a financial firm to pay the bills, but I wasn't happy, feeling that I could do more than just crunching numbers."

"I understand that feeling. So how did you get here in this shop?"

"The more I heard of others climbing to their Summit, the more I considered it. So two years ago, I took a break and made the climb."

"Wow. That is like my story."

"I had no idea it would lead me to fulfill my dream. My plan wasn't to stay here, but after I made the successful climb, the town woodcarver was retiring and looking to sell his business. I jumped at the chance and never looked back."

"What was it like to make it to the mountain top? How hard was it?"

"You'll make it. The people who quit are overconfident and lean on their own abilities and qualifications. You must depend on the team. Lack of trust is the biggest cause of failure."

"I've heard that before." Mallery recalled the chapter in the climbing booklet, **"Reasons for Failure**." "Are you speaking about the team I'll be training and climbing with?"

"Yes. Trust the training process. Fear and inaction can hold you back. Showing up, training, and getting on the mountain will put you ahead of those who quit before starting."

His words buoyed her spirits. "I need to believe these concepts and remember them at the right time." Her thoughts continued to spill out, "My own negative self-talk can sabotage me."

"The mind is powerful, but you've got all the necessary tools. Utilize them just like I do in this shop. The tools would only sit on the bench without my actions."

"That makes sense." Mallery continued, "By the way, what's that sign for?"

An expertly crafted circular sign hung on the wall with the words "Roundabout Hero."

"The previous owner left it. A woman ordered it years ago, but never picked it up. No one's asked about it until now."

"I may be interested."

"We ship all over the world. If you want it, let me know. I'll look forward to seeing you again and hearing of your success."

Mallery bounded toward her cottage and found dinner waiting for her. The welcoming warmth of a hot meal gave further assurance that she had made the right decision. After eating, she reread the paper contained with the emerald:

Finding this emerald should inspire you to keep going and never quit. You will need patience and perseverance in the days ahead, but you have everything within you to keep going. The secret is to grow and learn. If you have that mindset, you will reach your Summit. Defining your skills, experience, and what you love is a great start. Never, never quit. You will make it.

In her journal, she wrote:

Today I gave up my last jewel, the emerald. I may have spent too much time dwelling on the security it would bring, but I realize now the gems were given to me to invest. They helped me build a new future full of possibility.

That was all she could muster for now. Crockett was fast asleep, snoring in the corner. Smiling, she stroked him, knowing her faithful companion would be well cared for. She lay down on the small bed, setting her alarm for an early morning. She could not be late on her first day.

The next morning, the shopkeeper greeted her warmly. The training would begin with his instruction, then switch to the experienced climbers, who had already made the ascent. All six people in her group would climb in two groups of three. She brought her carabiners, hammer, pitons, and rope. The shopkeeper explained, "The climb will take three days. We'll furnish your sleeping bags, and you'll set up camp in caves carved in the mountainside."

Mallery couldn't keep quiet, "Three days?"

"It's a tall mountain!" This response immediately lightened the mood, so the instructions continued with how they would pack supplies and rely on each other. Her group seemed supportive. When Mallery was introduced, her name tag said "Andriette." She didn't have a chance to correct the mistake because the sessions were already starting. One of her team members reminded her of a colleague, named Bliss. That associate had been the one to first spark her interest in climbing to her Summit. Bliss acted kind and happy, yet smart and confident in what she wanted from life. Mallery would have to contact Bliss once she returned home. Taking on some of Bliss' attributes appealed to her.

The hours passed quickly as they not only had detailed instruction about dynamic and static ropes but also a lesson on team building. Rohan, the most experienced climber, took over the training.

"Your team will carry two types of ropes. You'll use the static rope the most as it provides very little stretch. But you'll also use a dynamic rope as it will stretch to absorb the impact of a fall."

Mallery felt the air getting sucked out of the room thinking about a fall. "Breathe in. Breathe out."

Rohan continued, "You don't need to worry. You will make a successful climb."

Multiple sized carabiners were passed around the room. The connectors would help them stay linked together as teammates. They'd depend on each other throughout their climb. Mallery kept so busy and engaged that she hadn't even looked outside. When they were dismissed for the day, she was surprised that it was already dark. Crockett met her at the cottage door with dog-kisses. Once again, a hot dinner was waiting for her. After eating, she collapsed on the bed, falling into a deep sleep but only after making sure her alarm was set for the next morning.

The following days held much of the same training, resulting in her bonding with her team. Everyone called her Andriette, and she hoped to live up to the name, as it meant "strong, fearless, and brave." Elana was extremely optimistic, which made sense as her name meant "light" or "moon" in some cultures. Rohan was one of the most patient guys she had ever met, so she enjoyed the training he provided. With a name that meant "ascending," she could see why he was so successful. She had never experienced relationships with those who were confident rather than doubtful and negative. Where could she find people like this in her small town? For the first time, she felt no need to prove that she belonged.

Each afternoon, Crockett met her with a load of enthusiasm, and she made sure to give him plenty of attention. On the last training day, they prepared for their climb the following morning. She had a new helmet, custom fit, lightweight, and sturdy. She had chosen a hard shell to provide the best protection. The little shop had everything they needed, including appropriate clothes. Mallery learned how to use all the climbing tools and even how to face challenging weather conditions while on the mountain. Just the night before she had written in her journal:

It feels like, in some ways, we are over-preparing for the climb, going over and over some of the same drills. But I'm realizing it is building confidence in me. I can positively do this. There's been so much training — more than I imagined. I don't want to let our team down.

That night, the team met for dinner. The shopkeeper asked what they hoped to achieve from their climbs. Elana had the dream of starting a nonprofit and said she wanted to face her fear of doing so. Others chimed in with similar messages, including the need to have a goal and work toward it.

"Andriette, what about you?" Mallery looked surprised, realizing the shopkeeper was calling on her. She was not used to her new name.

"At first, I just wanted to prove that I could be successful. But I found more on the way here. I want to reach my potential, to see what I'm capable of. Getting this far has expanded my vision for the future as it has helped me to focus on my strengths, and not how ill-fated I was."

There was silence. Then one of the team started clapping, and they all joined in, culminating with a big group hug.

"Tomorrow, be here bright and early. We will have a full day." Then the shopkeeper dismissed them for the night.

CHAPTER THIRTEEN

The Summit

Climbing day arrived. Mallery – now Andriette – had invested all she had to get to this point. She had journaled every evening, even the first night when so exhausted. Her last entry reflected her excitement:

The day has finally come. Tomorrow we begin climbing Hero Mountain. I'm more excited than fearful, which is a new feeling for me. I am with a team of people whom I trust and have grown to like. I don't want anything to keep me from getting to my Summit now. In a few days, I hope to reach the very top.

She had told her group about the Band of Hope around her wrist, and they all wanted one. She'd have to talk to her guide about that. Then she wondered where her guide was. He hadn't shown up here at all, which seemed strange. Maybe he would be at the top?

Her mind recalled the week she'd just had. In training, they practiced maneuvers up a virtual wall. Rohan scaled it like a monkey. Andriette watched him closely, drawing sketches for the rest of the team to picture the best placements for their feet and hands. This helped tremendously with everyone improving their performance. She had written:

I feel respected by my team as they followed my advice and were successful. I was even asked to interview for a job creating diagrams for a construction company after returning to Baybel.

That excited her, but for now, she wanted to focus on her Summit. Both teams arrived on time, ready and dressed for the climb with extra gear, sleeping bags, food, and emergency supplies. It was an hour drive to the starting point, so they set off once all members boarded the bus. What was Andriette feeling – part excitement and part apprehension with healthy fear in the mix? She knew their training was thorough and should equip them for any situation that might arise on the mountain, but there were still many unknowns. Though it was early, plenty of chatter filled the bus. Everyone felt anticipation for the adventure before them, so she didn't let her nervousness show. Her mind wandered back home. If her family and friends could only see her now. Craven, Shamere, Cagney, just thinking about them made her pity them. None of them would ever attempt a climb to their Summit.

"Okay everyone, grab your belongings!" Rohan made the climbers double and triple-check their supplies as there would be no turning back. As the bus left, they all faced the mountain before them. Andriette's nervousness had become a burst of adrenaline. Up close, the mountain looked steep. This was no climbing wall. The first segment of the climb was an unswerving vertical ascent. Both teams put on their helmets, wished each other luck, and assured their teammates they'd support each other.

As their team leader, Rohan went first and hammered the first piton into the rock. Luckily, Andriette could see that previous teams had left strategic pitons and pegs that extended from rocky crags farther up the surface. She strapped on her climbing harness and felt the firmness around her legs and waist. One of the main elements that they had covered in their daily instruction was how to trust and rely on their team. Her harness would serve as an added member of her team, providing a safe connection to the rope. Soon, they were all slowly making their way up the rocky mountainside. It was exhilarating to feel like she belonged to this group, especially after traveling alone for days. She could hear Elana's quiet conversation to herself. Listening to her kept Andriette looking towards the Summit, talking herself out of fear.

The full first day passed without incident, and it seemed much easier than she had anticipated. They had eaten their sack lunch midday and were now at the place where they would stay their first night. They found a flat rock big enough for all of them in a small cave-like opening with an overhang. With the wind and chill, she was glad for the extra jacket and layers she had brought. She was also grateful for the experience of the team leaders. They cooked a simple dinner with a single propane burner and discussed where they would each place their sleeping bags.

Nightfall revealed a million stars winking down at her, twinkling and unveiling the constellations she had only seen in books. She had never taken time to see the beauty of the night sky before. The vastness of the universe gave her new perspective as the expanse of the night sky reached forever in space. She was only one small speck in a single galaxy. Once again, she felt grateful to experience a trip of this significance. Daylight interrupted her dreams as she woke to realize the snoring next to her wasn't Crockett. It was cold, but she managed to coax her fingers, which were stiffer than usual, to write a few sentences in her journal before exiting her sleeping bag:

Our first day was exhilarating. It is refreshing and invigorating to be with a team of non-quitters. I hope the next two days are as exciting as the first.

She inhaled the rich aroma of coffee that was heating up on the single burner. Andriette looked out over the horizon, and even though she could feel the soreness of her muscles, the elevation, clean crisp air, and sense of adventure produced a high that coffee could never give. The chill of the night air had kept all their food cool and breakfast was simple with yogurt, berries, and granola. She did notice there was no roll and hoped Crockett was doing okay. The wind whipped up, so tucking her sleeping bag and belongings in her backpack was challenging, but they had all practiced packing many times thinking through different scenarios. They had talked about weather conditions in their training, now she realized why. The days had been so beautiful and clear before they left, but on the mountain side, weather patterns changed quickly.

"Nothing to worry about. We'll continue on," Rohan assured them. "Andriette, you lead."

Thinking of herself as Andriette, she responded quickly. She checked her supplies and slipped into her climbing harness. The first section didn't look as difficult as what they had scaled the day before, so she was glad this was her segment for leading. She hammered a piton in the rock and took two steps up, thankful that her climbing shoes gripped the rock with sticky rubber soles. It didn't seem that challenging until a strong blast of wind took her by surprise, making her drop her hammer. She clung to the mountain, frozen, scared to move. The rope beneath her started to lurch and flap with every gust. She could feel her heart beating faster, and her breathing coming in gusts with the wind. She looked down, trying to see where her hammer went, but she could not will herself to look up. She had the vision, once again, of hanging off the bridge, wondering if she should just give up. Yet doing so would hold the whole team back.

Suddenly, her teammates shouted, "Look up! Look up!" But she couldn't hear anything except the flurry of wind around her. Her own thoughts of falling made her deaf to their cries. Her body shook, both from the wind and her growing fear. Was she experiencing a panic attack? Another gust hit even harder, sending her closer to the rock. She could see her wrist and her fingers, now tightly gripped on the rock with knuckles that had turned white. The Band of Hope felt solid, but she couldn't look at it. She was stuck on the side of a mountain with a strong wind pushing her into the rock. She closed her eyes and tried to remember that same hope she had felt when the band was recovered at the café, but it wouldn't come.

"Look up, look up," she heard. Opening her eyes, she saw beautiful wings flutter close and land on her shoulder, which surprised her enough to make her look to her side. A magnificent butterfly rested close to her face. Then it lifted off slowly, floating in the wind, and her eyes followed its motion until she was looking up. It held a remarkable resemblance to the butterfly she had seen emerge from its cocoon. It stayed, flitting in circles above her as if to keep her focused. She slowed her breathing. "Breathe in. Breathe out."

"You're doing great, Andriette. Keep looking up." Her teammates bolstered her confidence and hope, just like the small act of kindness from the barista, who didn't even know her. She now knew there was a reason her guide had given her the small elastic band, to remember why she came on this journey and why she needed hope to succeed. She was on the climb of her life. No one else could climb for her. She had to do it herself. And she had to keep her hope alive to make it. Slowly, she took her next step and her next and her next, inching up the mountain.

"That's it, that's it, Andriette!"

She *was* good enough. The voices of her teammates echoed around her as they cheered her on. Tears filled her eyes. She was doing it! Braving the elements, pushing through her fear. She had to do this by herself, yet she wasn't alone. She had teammates – trusted friends. They were calling her Andriette. While they were training, they spoke often of lifting each other up. They would not leave anyone stranded on a cliff. If one person was injured, they would all pull together to get that teammate to safety.

She heard Rohan's voice beneath her, "Andriette, take my hammer!"

Andriette had never experienced this kind of support. Rohan wanted her to keep leading. She had written about the respect she felt from her team, but this act affirmed it. Her guide had given her the same reassurance, showing up when she needed him. She now would have the strength to finish what she started. With his hammer, she continued up the mountain with intent and resolve. Her teammates followed right behind her. The wind continued with stronger gusts, but their small team kept on. The magnificent butterfly stayed by Andriette all day as her traveling companion, steadying her mind. Before the sun fully disappeared beyond the landscape, they reached the crevice where they would camp for the night. The sky became a magnificent shade of pink, orange, purple and yellow. Their landing place, consisting of large flat rocks, was large enough for both teams to land in a cave that would protect them from the wind.

"Why wouldn't everyone want to see this?" It was a question Andriette was asking mostly of herself, but two teammates were voicing the same question, marveling at the beauty before them. Andriette had rarely stopped long enough to view many sunsets. Even when she did, she never spent enough time to enjoy them like she was now. Never again. Her perspective had changed. This trip had done more than just help her reach her Summit. It had given her confidence in who she was and who she could really become.

After the sun set, a full moon made its ascent. Both teams had eaten their packed dinners in silence, and one team member uncovered an extra hammer in the emergency supplies, which he gave to Andriette. Without thinking, she began singing:

I've been on a journey; this is my Summit song. I'm almost to the top. Now it won't be long.

She was surprised when a few others joined her. Then the whole team sang together as a chorus,

We've been on a journey; this is our Summit song. We're almost to the top. Now it won't be long.

The sound echoed off the mountain, no one caring how they sounded as they huddled together to view the beauty before them. She flicked on her reading light and wrote in her journal:

If all goes as planned, we will reach the Summit tomorrow. I wonder if it's possible to feel any more alive than I do right now. I had accepted the fact that even if I never got this far, my life has changed in many ways. I am excited about pursuing a new future, using more of my skills, and reaching out to true friends. But the fact that I will get to the top is truly miraculous and my life will never be the same.

With that, she slipped into her sleeping bag and drifted into a deep, peaceful sleep.

The next morning was like the other days on the mountain except that Andriette was going to reach her Summit. Unless one of their team members got hurt, there was no reason they shouldn't all get there by early afternoon. Even if something happened to keep them from their destination, Andriette had all she needed. Her life had changed for the better. Both teams were chattering excitedly, gulping down quick cups of coffee while eating their morning fuel of granola and yogurt. The peak of the mountain lay in a low cloud layer, but the weather looked clear. The other team left first. As they rolled up their sleeping bags and packed their supplies, they began singing:

We've been on a journey; this is our Summit song.
We're almost to the top. Now it won't be long.

They laughed as their dissonant notes bounced off the mountain. The first team would leave first to climb on the other side of a large crevice where the rock split into sections.

"Both sides should be about the same difficulty," Rohan instructed as their team made sure all their gear was packed correctly. Andriette watched him take additional time to check his ropes and connections. They gave fist bumps and hugs before strapping into their harnesses. Andriette couldn't see the exact route the other team had taken, but to her, the side they would climb looked more difficult. She was grateful when Rohan said, "I'll go first." She would follow, and Elana would bring up the rear. Today, they would be connected closer together as this last section was slick and straight up the mountain. As Rohan started, loose pebbles and dust flew down with every step. They could see his foot slide several times.

"I'm okay. It's just slippery." Andriette grabbed the rope and motioned to Elana. "You can go next if you'd like."

Elana responded with a smile, "No, I'm good!" Andriette double-checked the tension of her rope, making sure all connections were secure. She put extra chalk on her hands, now sweaty, and grabbed the rope. She knew it was the rock that was slippery and not the rope, but the chalk made her feel more secure. Both she and Elana would depend on Rohan's anchors, though they could both hammer in their own pitons if needed. With Rohan leading, they felt confident they would get past this section by noon. They were soon making good progress, though Andriette let out a squeal when she placed a finger-hold in a crevice and a bird flew out. She looked all around as she climbed, dismissing the tightness in her shoulders and arms. Elana was humming below her.

"Whoa!" Rohan shouted as suddenly his rope jerked down and both Andriette and Elana descended several feet.

"Aaah!" Screams came from both women.

Rohan yelled, "The anchor's not holding!" Their screams were amplified with the next free-fall as they dangled several feet away from the mountain. They all hung on the rope, knowing their lives depended on the intertwined fibers. The moment lasted seconds but felt like minutes. Andriette wasn't the only one looking down; they were all focused on the possibility of a fall that would surely end any future. Her screams came involuntarily. Not even a butterfly would help today. When she momentarily looked up, she saw Rohan trying to reach a crevice to place another anchor, but it was out of his reach.

"Quiet! Calm down!" Rohan's voice bounced off the mountain, then immediate silence, with the sound of her breathing and the whistling of the wind. Still, it was deafening.

"Everyone, stay still!" Andriette was surprised at her calm command.

Rohan's rope slipped again, and they all abruptly dropped another ten feet. Andriette's toes clenched, and she brought her legs into her stomach for comfort, as if in a yoga child's pose. She closed her eyes, hanging in a freeform swing apart from the mountain. She needed to think. Andriette slowly looked up. The pose helped her relax the tightness in her back, and she could see the current piton was not going to hold. But she could also imagine the climbing wall with its handholds and footholds.

"Rohan, there's a pattern. The crevice to your right will hold – I know it. Can you reach it?"

"No!" She could hear the panic in Rohan's voice, which was not reassuring.

"I can see where we need to go. If we all swing to the right, Rohan can place a solid anchor in the crevice."

Elana couldn't help herself, "I'll be the first to die!" They knew if one fell, they would all fall.

"Stop, Elana! You can't think that way. Let's focus and do this together. Think of this as a climbing wall." Andriette had no idea where her burst of strength was coming from, but the Band of Hope tightened around her wrist.

"I can see the pattern. You need to trust me. We all have to swing together and push far enough away from the wall to get Rohan to the crevice."

She wished Elana would demonstrate Crockett's calmness when crossing the bridge, but her teammate's panic furthered Andriette's determination to get them through this crisis.

"I'm going to count down from three, and on one, everyone, swing to the right. Got it?" There was no answer, but Andriette took that as "yes."

"Okay. Three, two, one, swing!" Andriette could feel the weight of Elana beneath her, "Elana, you have to move!"

Her command awakened Elana from her panic. "We have to do it again. Three, two, one, swing!" This time they started swinging slowly, then they heard Rohan celebrate.

"I've got it! I've got it!" Rohan grabbed the wall and pushed the anchor in, then firmly secured it with a swing of the hammer and attached a carabiner. Andriette felt a rush of gratitude. "Now a foot up and just to your left." Still looking up, Andriette kept giving commands, as both she and Elana followed Rohan, inserting their own pitons for safety. They moved up slowly, all clinging close to the rock for the rest of the day. She heard Elana talking softly and humming, which reassured her. Time didn't matter now; only safety and getting to the next level. When they found themselves at the place where they had slept the previous night, they realized how far they had fallen. They had lost a whole day but gained perspective and respect for the mountain. It would be just the three of them for the night, but they knew the other team would be waiting for them. According to their emergency plan, one of them could climb up for help, but they felt that would be unnecessary. Their dinner would be protein bars, nuts, and water, for food was the least of their concerns.

"What went wrong?" Elana asked the big question.

"It was my mistake." Rohan admitted, "a dislodged anchor could happen to anyone. But there was erosion around the crevice, and I questioned the placement of the anchor, but I got in a hurry. Overconfidence was my mistake."

Andriette remembered what the Willow and Birch shopkeeper had said, "The people who don't make it are overconfident and lean entirely on their own abilities and qualifications."

But Rohan continued, "I was thinking about getting to the top and wasn't calculating the weight of the team. I learned a valuable lesson today." It was refreshing that even someone at Rohan's climbing level was learning.

Elana chimed in, "I fell into the same trap and found myself willing to give up until Andriette yelled at me. I was in it for the ride up today, thinking it would be easy, but I had to pull my own weight to get out of the mess." They all sat in silence, relishing the quiet and the protection the crevice gave them for the night. Most of the stars were hidden, but the full moon kept appearing between the clouds. Andriette took out her journal:

Tonight is different than last night. It's so quiet. I am thankful to be sitting here in a safe place, given what could have happened today. If one of us had fallen, we would all have gone down as we were all attached to the rope. But the team listened to me when I felt like it could be the end. I could visualize stepping-stones up the mountain, just like the climbing wall, and spoke up knowing they would not think it was a crazy idea. Rohan was the one who had to make sure each place was secure, but I knew he'd keep us as safe as possible. I've never experienced being on a team like this. We had to trust each other to survive.

She didn't want to disturb Rohan and Elana who were both in their sleeping bags gazing up at the sky, as though they were reflecting. She wrote more:

Finishing a trip like this has taken more than I ever imagined. It has not only taken physical strength I didn't know I had, but a mental determination I had to muster when I wanted to give up. I've not thought about the jewels the whole time I've been on the mountain, which is surprising. But I know now they were given to me so I could gain what I've achieved right here. My life will never be the same. I needed to discover for myself that I was good enough all along. I hope to find more people like Rohan and Elana who will be the types of friends not to let me quit.

The next morning was colder, but the wind died down. Rohan had the burner in his supplies to make coffee, so they had cups to warm their hands and their insides. Through the clouds and mist, they looked at the same section they had started yesterday. Rohan spoke first, "You can't let yesterday's setback influence today. You'll be able to see the right path ahead. We'll take it slowly to reach the top."

Elana said, "I'll go first, today." Andriette was glad. Elana had more carabiners than usual clipped to her belt. Andriette smiled to herself thinking it was quite the fashion statement, but quickly regained her focus as she saw what stood before them. The face of the mountain looked even more steep, and she hoped her rock shoes would grip on the moist stone. But she had to trust it was safe.

Rohan grabbed the rope and motioned to Andriette, "You want to go next?"

"No, you go." Pebbles flew down from Elana's shoes, but Andriette could see she was double-checking every anchor before connecting.

Rohan clipped in and called out, "You're good, Elana. I'm right behind you."

Watching Rohan was not encouraging as his foot slipped twice, and he hadn't even made it halfway up the initial ascent. Andriette, with less experience, worried as her teammate was slipping above her. She started humming then singing softly,

We've been on a journey; this is our Summit song.
We're almost to the top. Now it won't be long.
We've been on a journey; this is our Summit song.
We're almost to the top. Now it won't be long.

Elana was getting close to the section where they had fallen the day before, so Rohan called down, looking at her.

"Start clipping in, Andriette!" Rohan's foot slipped again, showering her with dust. "Don't let that scare you. You'll be all right. Just clip in!"

The peak was so close that she couldn't quit now. Yet overcoming this last stretch looked hard, especially mentally. She had given everything to be here, but could she make it? Both Elana and Rohan now called down, "Remember to look up, Andriette. You can do this!" Andriette thought of the message included with the emerald:

```
Finding this emerald should inspire you to keep going
and never quit. Never, never quit. You will make it!
```

She said it out loud, "Never, never quit. Never, never quit." She couldn't let her teammates down just like she couldn't leave Crockett at the cave. "I'm coming!" Her voice sounded confident while she made sure her carabiner, rope, and harness were secure. With her first steps, her arm slammed against the rock as her foot slid down, barely finding a small shelf in the granite. Her arm, barely healed from her bridge fall, throbbed with pain. In fact, her whole body hurt. Then she saw it.

"Hello butterfly! You came back!" Vibrant wings fluttered about her face, then circled straight toward the top.

She looked up. Both Rohan and Elana shouted, "That's it, Andriette, look up!"

They thought their words made the difference, but seeing the butterfly was another magical occurrence to help her. The Band of Hope felt secure as she ascended a few more steps. Then, she slipped on the slick rock. Ignoring her thumping heart, throbbing arm pain, and leg stiffness, she kept on. Time slowed down. It was one anchor, one grip, and one step at a time as the team of three pulled themselves up the side of the mountain. Andriette heard voices and squinted. The other team was waiting for them at the top. Although her arms shook in exhaustion, she felt determined. The sun broke through the clouds. The butterfly's wings shone a vibrant beacon of light ahead of her.

"Keep it up, Andriette! You're doing great!" Rohan stayed far enough ahead to bolster her confidence. If he could make it, she could, too. The other team kept cheering them on. The burst of adrenaline she felt at the bottom of the mountain was nothing compared to now. She was going to the top!

Once both Elana and Rohan reached the peak, they joined their voices with the others.

"Andriette, Andriette, you're almost here. You're strong and brave. The Summit is near! Andriette, Andriette, you're almost here. You're strong and brave. The Summit is near!" Her teammates all lay flat on the rock with arms extended to pull her up. Now, as Andriette, she counted her steps, just like on the bridge. One, two, three, four… ten, eleven… then with one huge push, she hoisted herself to the top ledge, holding on to the rock with her right hand, the Band of Hope hugging her arm. With her left hand, she grabbed the fingers reaching out to her. Multiple hands then grabbed her wrists and helped her pull herself up the rope with one last forceful effort.

Everyone cheered loudly. They had all done it, reached their Summit. Now, her tears flowed in a flood. This was the physical Summit, but she had reached a personal Summit days before. The mountaintop symbolized her accomplishment. All the climbers stood to view the massive valley below. She couldn't see Baybel in the distance, for it symbolized a much smaller part of her life. Looking beyond the Summit, she saw higher peaks, some even snow covered. In fact, she saw another climber who looked familiar. Was it her guide? Or maybe the shopkeeper?

There would be more mountains to climb, more lessons to learn and more adventure to discover. The last chapter in the book on climbing, "**Regular Maintenance**," would be her guide, reminding her to maintain a healthy mindset and outlook. That would prove more valuable than all the jewels she had gathered. She had come full circle. Now, she was good enough as Andriette, not only in reaching her Summit but also in realizing the strength within her. She had everything she needed.

Epilogue

After celebrating at the mountain top, the teams made their way down the other side. Andriette felt exhausted but exhilarated to find a gondola just beyond the next ridge. It descended through a beautiful, lush pass culminating at the far end of the town where a bus stood waiting. Back at the shop, the climbers sat in a circle in the same place where they had trained. Each member was wearing a yellow Band of Hope wristband, waiting for them upon their return. Andriette had returned to the Willow and Birch shop where the shopkeeper gave her the "Roundabout Hero" sign. Happy to see her, Crockett wolfed down bowls of food. The dog sitter explained that some pets hardly eat while their owners are away but make up for it upon their owners' return.

The shopkeeper asked, "What did you gain from your trip, besides the exhilaration of getting to the top?"

Rohan spoke first, "I had a huge wake-up call. I've been doing this for a long while. But I let overconfidence rule, and it almost culminated in disaster. Thankfully, my team stuck with me. We slowed down enough to make the climb safely. A special thanks to Andriette. She should be an instructor for the climbing wall." This suggestion brought laughter as others chimed in.

Elana added, "Starting a nonprofit seems much easier now after climbing Hero Mountain. It's one hand and one foot at a time. I can't wait to begin the process on solid ground."

After more laughter, Andriette stood. She pretended to be in front of hundreds of people sharing her ideas. She held the "Roundabout Hero" sign as she spoke, "I know better than ever what I can do. The fact that Rohan trusted my instructions after we fell meant a lot." She looked directly at him and smiled. "But even more, I was elated that my directions worked." Rohan smiled back. She looked around the room, "I'm not afraid any more to pursue new possibilities and ideas."

"What's the sign for?" Rohan asked.

"Until I focused on my greater purpose in getting here, I circled needlessly on what felt like an endless roundabout of distraction." While holding everyone's attention, she kept going, "Once I let go of superficial goals and desires, I saw a clear, forward path called 'Roundabout Hero.' I can't forget why I came and from where I came."

Everyone stood to link arms for one last cheer. Andriette knew she was no longer ill-fated but instead was strong, fearless, and brave. Her potential felt limitless. Her crazy ideas were worth pursuing and that was worth the climb on the road to success, achievement, and satisfaction. She had reached her Summit.

About the Author

Deborah Johnson, M.A. is an author, composer, and performer, having published several books and released multiple albums, along with writing hundreds of songs and three full-length musicals. In addition, she produces a popular podcast, *Women at Halftime*. Her books include *Stuck is Not a Four Letter Word, Bad Code: Overcoming Bad Mental Code that Sabotages Your Life, Music for Kids,* and *Women at Halftime*. Deborah grew up reading every fairy tale she could get her hands on and relishes the creative process. Along with writing, she enjoys the outdoors and traveling with her husband. She loves spending time with her children and grandchildren as well.

Up for multiple **GRAMMY Awards** and spending over 20 years in the entertainment industry, she's built multiple self-driven businesses. **Deborah** speaks and performs for both live and virtual events, using her uniqueness and skills to help others climb their summits.

CPSIA information can be obtained
at www.ICGtesting.com
Printed in the USA
BVHW051209210921
617186BV00002B/137

9 781733 348423